THE BOOK OF THE SWORD

THE BOOK OF THE SWORD

A. J. LAKE

SPECIAL THANKS TO LINDA CAREY

BLOOMSBURY

First published in Great Britain in 2007 by Bloomsbury Publishing Plc
36 Soho Square, London, W1D 3QY

A CIP catalogue record of this book is available from the British Library

ISBN 978 0 7475 8632 6

All papers used by Bloomsbury Publishing are natural, recyclable products made
from wood grown in well-managed forests. The manufacturing processes conform to
the environmental regulations of the country of origin.

Typeset by RefineCatch Ltd, Bungay, Suffolk
Printed in Great Britain by Clays Ltd, St Ives Plc

1 3 5 7 9 10 8 6 4 2

www.darkestage.com
www.bloomsbury.com

PROLOGUE

The walls of the cave were of stone and ice, but fire blazed at its heart. A deep crack snaked through the rocky ground, its dull red depths pulsing in time with the rumbling that filled the air. At the heart of the cave, molten rock had escaped from the earth below, pooling in a hollow filled with glowing fire. And over the hollow, red-lit in the gloom, was a great slab of black basalt, forming a makeshift anvil. The clang of a hammer mingled with the growling of the earth, and made the black rock shake.

The smith, a short, barrel-chested man, struck tirelessly at the strip of metal before him. He might have been fifty: his thick hair and beard were grey, but his powerful build and bright eyes suggested that he had lost little of his strength. He glowered down at his work, hunching jealously over the glowing strip before him.

The hammer's clangs became higher and sharper, then mere taps, as the metal faded from brilliant white to red, and the smith took a step backwards, letting out his breath in a great sigh.

'Is it done?'

A young woman stepped forward from the cavern's edge. She could have been a part of the cave's ice and shadow: slender and black-haired, her skin almost as colourless as the white shift she wore – but her face was bright with eagerness.

The smith raised his lined face and looked full at the woman for the first time.

'It's shaped,' he said heavily. 'You're resolved on this?'

'Yes!' Her voice was fierce.

'It's time, then.' The smith knelt for a moment by his primitive forge. On the ground, scratched in the basalt of the cave floor, was a rough circle a few arm's-lengths wide, and in it lay an intricately wrought metal gauntlet. He raised the gauntlet as delicately as if it were glass, turning it in his hands with a craftsman's pride. Even in the dimness, out of the fire's glow, the gauntlet seemed to glitter, its hundreds of tiny links reflecting the light like fish-scales. The smith sighed again, and slipped the gauntlet on to his right hand, where it fitted like a second skin.

He got to his feet and picked up the still-smoking sword, his shoulders tensing as if it were unexpectedly heavy. He stood for an instant breathing deeply – then raised the blade in the air and stepped into the stone circle.

The woman crossed swiftly to join him. As she entered the circle she began to chant, low at first but raising her voice to a shrill keening, her eyes fixed on the firelit blade. The song came to an end, and she bowed her head. At the same instant the old man lowered the sword so that the point brushed her chest, above her heart. He hesitated, and she reached out with both hands to grasp the smoking blade and pull it towards her, one sharp tug that lasted for ever and less than a heart-beat.

There was a sudden hissing sound and the woman's face contorted in agony, though it was the old man who cried out, still holding fast to the sword's hilt. Her blood ran down the blade, falling in red drops on to her white dress. The two faced each other across the circle, surrounded by wreaths of steam from the hissing blade. Gradually the woman's face relaxed, and now clear light was welling from beneath her hands, stealing along the sword and spreading like frost along her bare arms. The light filled the stone circle till it blazed like the sun, sending shadows fleeing to the distant ice walls. The woman was calm now, smiling faintly. She seemed suddenly transparent, as if the light shone through her.

There was a rush and clatter of footsteps, and a man burst into the cave.

'*No!*'

He was young by the sound of his voice, and desperate, though hardly to be seen in the blackness around the sword's glare. He hurled himself towards the circle – and staggered back as if the dazzling light were a barrier. He beat at it with his fists, soundlessly.

'Please!' he howled. 'Take me instead!'

From inside the circle the woman turned her head to look

at him, her smile touched with regret. Her body seemed transfixed, and strangely insubstantial in the unravelling light. When she spoke it was barely more than a whisper.

'You could not . . . Can only be me.'

She was shimmering now, her skin wavering into motes of light. Only her eyes stayed fixed on the unseen figure for a moment longer, dark and clear.

'Goodbye . . . my love . . .'

The sword's light was dying, and she faded with it; her body drifted into smoke that swirled briefly around the still-glowing sword. Then the sword itself began to disappear; motes of light sinking into the surface of the blade and vanishing; the blade becoming insubstantial. Once again the cave was lit only by the dull glow of the fires under the earth; even the molten rock beneath the forge had retreated, leaving the great slab of stone dark and bare. And the two who remained had no words for each other: the young man sobbing on his knees, and the old one, staring in disbelief and terror at his empty right hand.

CHAPTER ONE

I knew even then that the fiery light in the north meant war. But I could not know how much that war would take from me. [*The Book of the Sword*]

Elspeth screamed.

A remembered agony shot through her right arm, and with it a sense of overwhelming grief and loss. In the blackness behind her eyelids the vision persisted – the young man kneeling, head bent; the old man staring horrified at his bare hand, both bathed in red light. And the scene stirred memories of her own: of another fire-lit cave; a metal gauntlet found in a sea-wracked chest, and the sword that had sprung so unexpectedly to her own hand. In her strange dream, she knew she had seen the forging of the crystal sword – the blade that was as much a part of her now as her own arm. But who was the young woman – not so much older than Elspeth herself, perhaps – who had played such a willing part in the painful ritual, and had disappeared?

Her arm still throbbed; hurting worse now than it had in the dream. Elspeth suddenly realised that both her arms were pinned painfully to her sides, and she could not feel her legs at all. Was she in prison again? Had the sorcerer Orgrim recaptured her? But surely she and Edmund had escaped, had defeated Orgrim. They had been feasted by the King of Wessex himself . . . hadn't they?

A gust of cold stung her face, and she opened her eyes . . . to find nothing but freezing mist, whipping around her in an unseen wind. She might have been back on her father's ship, carving a path through a winter blizzard – were it not for the way she was gripped, feet dangling, her arms clamped to her body by two great, scaled talons.

Memory scorched back: the dragon! It had ripped the roof off the king's hall; seized her and Edmund . . . Elspeth's heart was suddenly knocking so hard that she could hear it, and there seemed no air to breathe. Biting down on a cry of panic, she peered desperately through the greyness for any sign of Edmund. But there was nothing. The suffocating fog pressed against her on all sides, and she was entirely alone.

No. Never alone.

The voice filled her head and ran through her nerves like lightning. Her arm was throbbing again: looking down, she saw the familiar light of the crystal sword in her right hand, pale and indistinct at first, but growing stronger, more brilliant as she watched.

Beneath her, as if dispelled by the sword's light, the fog had begun to clear. Elspeth could see land far below: an indistinct expanse of white and black glimpsed through swirls of mist. A moment later the last of the mist had gone, replaced by clear blue sky and the dazzling rays of an early morning sun. The dragon had been flying inside a cloud, Elspeth realised. Below her now was a landscape of ice and snow, barred with soft light. To one side lay a swathe of stippled darkness that might be a forest; to the other, the sun was just showing its face between mountains white with snow, their tops pink-lit by the dawn sky.

I am with you until our task is done.

What task? Elspeth wondered. What was she expected to do, in this alien land? Did the sword have some plan for her, even now? The blade's glow in her hand seemed to pulse, like the heartbeat of a living thing, and a sudden suspicion seized her: *the sword wanted me here.*

What are you doing to me? she demanded. *Did you bring me here?*

The voice in her head was silent.

Answer me! she insisted.

This is where we must be, the voice said at last. *But not like this – not carried in the dragon's claws.* And a sudden terror filled her: the sword's fear that, after all, the great plan would fail – if Elspeth could not free herself.

'*What* plan?' In her exasperation, Elspeth had spoken aloud, but the wind whipped her words away before her ears could hear them. At that moment the beast holding her banked, tilting her sickeningly sideways as it veered towards the mountains, and she saw Edmund.

He was hanging limply from the dragon's other front claw, too far away to call to, even without the whistling wind in her ears. From this angle she could see little but his white-blond hair and the once-fine blue cloak, now hanging around him in tatters. His head hung down as if he were unconscious, and what she could see of his face was as pale as his linen shirt.

There was a flicker of movement in the air above him, and Elspeth's gaze flashed in alarm to the great blue-scaled foreleg that held him. It was as thick around as an oak, double-jointed like a lizard's and folded back against the great barred underbelly that filled the sky above her. The sheer size of the creature that held them made her shudder afresh, but there *was* something moving there, something small and fast, even higher up. She twisted her neck painfully, scanning up and along the blue-black mass to where it joined the body . . . There. A tiny brown figure was clinging to the dragon's shoulder. No, not tiny: a grown man, with a rope around his waist and a sword in his belt – who looked down and jerked his head in greeting.

Cathbar!

She had no time to wonder how the captain came to be there. He had passed his rope right around the dragon's great

12

forelimb: his perch was precarious, but he had both arms free as he signalled her. He pointed to the snowy ground far below, making opening and closing gestures with one hand. Then he drew his sword.

Elspeth understood him at once, and her first response was: *No!* He could not attack the dragon in flight! The fall would kill them, all three. But Cathbar was gesturing again, his face impatient. She looked down again. They were much closer to the ground than before. The black clumps below were recognisable as trees; she could even see the snow on their top branches. But Edmund still dangled unconscious from the dragon's claw – how could he survive?

Cathbar pointed again, straight ahead this time. She followed his gesture – and suddenly understood. They were heading for the mountains. Jagged cliffs of grey stone loomed ahead of them: there would be no surviving *that* fall. And if they did not fight – if the dragon were allowed to take them to its master . . . whoever that was. Orgrim had been blinded and driven mad, so *who summoned Torment now?* One thing was for certain – this was no friend or ally who had sent the dragon to snatch them from Beotrich's hall.

She forced her gaze back to Cathbar, and nodded once.

Smoothly, without a moment's wait, the man swung himself into the hollow of the dragon's shoulder and stabbed upwards. The first stroke brought barely a shudder to the claw holding Elspeth, but a low rumbling began to shake the air around her. At the second stroke a great convulsion whipped

13

Elspeth through the air like a fish on a line. White earth and blue air whirled around her while above the great throat pulsed with an agonised roar. Out of the corner of one eye she saw a tree-like limb flailing through the air; saw Edmund, released, drop like a wounded bird.

She had time to breathe a few words of a prayer for Edmund's life before another convulsion shook her. Bucking and plunging in the air, she saw the fight in flashes: a gout of black blood oozing from the dragon's chest; Cathbar, the rope only holding his feet, leaning dangerously far over the beast's shoulder as he tried to strike closer to the throat. Then the great head swung round, cutting off her view.

For an instant, as the dragon tried to reach its own chest, Elspeth caught sight of its cavernous mouth; the smoking pit of a nostril, and then the huge eye filled her sight. She could swear the eye focused on her, filled with a cold and terrifying hatred: *you won't escape me!*

'Sword!' she whispered desperately, and the sword seemed to writhe in her hand, pulsing in rhythm with her own blood. But she could not move her arm to lift it. The claw gripping her was clenched so tightly that she could hardly breathe.

The dragon had found the source of its pain. The great head snaked upwards, sending a jet of blue flame along its shoulder. Cathbar hurled himself out of the way, his clothes burning; the scorched end of the rope whipped through the air as the dragon drew its head back to swat him into the sky.

Before her vision was cut off Elspeth caught one last glimpse of him, lunging forward for a final blow.

The dragon screamed – and the talon gripping Elspeth slackened its grasp. Her arm was so numb she hardly knew how she moved it, but she managed a wild swipe at the limb above her head. Below her she saw Cathbar falling, a trail of blue fire following him like the tail of a comet. And then she was plunging after him, rolling over and over in the air, the sword flashing and the wind whistling about her, until the world went white.

CHAPTER TWO

They came to my door in winter: three of them. By their manner, and their height, I knew they were of the Fay.

They knew that my mortal father had been a smith, before their people stole me – and they called me by the name the Fay had given me: Brokk, the dwarf, because I was so much shorter than their people. They spoke, too, of things I had thought the Fay would want forgotten: how they cast me out when I grew up, the iron in my blood proving too strong for them; and how I took with me their fairest daughter as my wife.

– What do you want of me? I asked them.

– We need you to forge a sword, they said.

Edmund opened his eyes on a dazzling pale-blue sky. Uneven white walls rose all about him and cold stung his face. His hand clenched in something soft and freezing: snow! He was lying on his back in snow – deeper than he had ever known in his life, for he seemed to have burrowed into it. Where was he?

He tried to sit up and pain shot through him, followed by panic as the walls of snow began to collapse. A soft, heavy mass poured down on him, and he scrabbled to get free, flapping both hands frantically above his head as the stuff covered his face. The rest of his body was covered by the time he finally got his head clear, coughing out the snow that had found its way into his mouth and nose. He was in a white wasteland, stretching as far as he could see in one direction; bordered by dark trees in another. Straight ahead of him, the sun was rising between bare, jagged mountains. It was all so strange that for a moment he simply lay there, just looking.

And then he saw the dragon.

It came at him out of nowhere, a giant, sinuous shape, its scales glittering blue-black in the pale air. He recognised it at once: Torment. Torment, the enemy of men, who had set him on this strange path when it destroyed Elspeth's ship and her father . . . and now it had plucked him out of the king's hall in Venta Bulgarum, when he'd been so near to home. He remembered the sickening lurch up into the dark; the despair that had gripped him. Had it come back to finish him? The creature swooped low, only a few feet above him it seemed: he could feel the malice in the vast, cold eye. The eye itself seemed damaged in some way, streaked with black, but Edmund would never forget the threat of that stare. Terror caught in his throat, and he dug his hands into the snow as if he could cover himself again.

But the dragon did not strike. With a sound like a thunder-crack, the great wings whipped down, and the long body rose into the sky in a rush of wind. The creature flapped away towards the mountains, huge and ungainly, with one foreleg hanging awkwardly down. In a few heartbeats it had vanished among the peaks.

The relief that flooded Edmund made him too weak to move for a while. He gazed at the mountains, his eyes swimming in the cold and the strengthening light of the sun. Dawn. It had been evening when the dragon took him and Elspeth, the lamps not long lit. So they must have been flying all night – and judging by the countryside, they'd gone north, far north. This land was wilder even than his father's stories of Hibernia. But why had Torment dropped him here? And was Elspeth here too?

Elspeth! He remembered now the creature's trailing leg and scarred eye. Elspeth must have got loose somehow, and used the crystal sword. Please, gods, let her have jumped safely herself; let her still be alive . . . He pulled himself half out of the snow, sending a spray of flakes into the air as he fought to get free. His legs were numb, and the rest of him hurt fiercely, as if he were bruised all over. He ignored the dull ache, dug down into the snow with his hands to free his legs and hauled himself up. The snow crumbled beneath him as he rolled into a sitting position, rubbing at his legs and wincing as the feeling came back in little hot stabs. It was hard to stand up; his knees kept buckling and the snow offered no purchase, but he managed it at last, shivering as he cast about him for any sign of movement.

At first, there was nothing. The white waste stretched away in all directions, level and bare. The sun, now risen above the mountains, dazzled his eyes, and he turned away from it to scan the distant forest. Was that a speck of light against the dark trees? He blinked and stared again. Yes: the snow in that direction rose into a hummock, with a scuffed-looking area halfway down, and in the middle of it a bright streak moved, as if waving to him . . .

His feet slipped and sank in the powdery snow as he started to run. He fell a dozen times, sinking to his waist in one particularly deep drift. But before he was halfway there he saw it clearly. It was the crystal sword, blazing as it caught the low light, and – praise the gods – Elspeth was struggling out of the snow behind it, using the point of the blade to steady herself.

She saw him as he approached, and started towards him, stumbling as much as he did. When they reached each other she caught him in a clumsy, one-armed hug.

'I thought you must be dead!' she whispered. Her face was wet against his; whether with tears or snow he could not tell.

'I was afraid *you* were! What are we doing here, Elspeth? Why would the dragon take us to a place like this?'

She shook her head. 'I don't know. I'm afraid that the sword . . .' She trailed off unhappily. 'I think something here wants the sword, and sent the dragon to get it. If it hadn't dropped us . . .'

'How *did* it drop us? You used the sword . . . ?'

'No!' Elspeth insisted. 'I didn't do anything – it was Cathbar.' Her eyes widened and she started up, away from him. 'Edmund, we have to find him!'

'Cathbar! But how . . . ?'

'I think he tied himself to the dragon's tail before it took us.' Elspeth's voice was unsteady. 'He stood on its back, and fought it . . . and it burned him, and he fell . . .'

She had started to shake. Edmund squeezed her arm, trying to keep the anxiety from his own face. 'The fall didn't kill *us* – he'll be alive somewhere,' he said, more confidently than he felt. 'We'll find him.'

Elspeth nodded, visibly controlling herself. 'At least we have light to search by,' she said. 'But the snow's so deep . . .'

'We don't have to look for him!' Edmund cut in. 'Well, not like that!'

A few short weeks ago he had been ashamed of his gift – so recently, and painfully, discovered. The Ripente, the seers through others' eyes, were too often viewed as spies and traitors. But without the gift, neither of them would be alive now. Almost with eagerness, he sank down cross-legged in the snow, closed his eyes, and cast out his sight.

Nothing close. Nothing at all in the waste of snow to his left, or the mountains behind him. To his relief, there was not even a flicker of the dragon's awareness. He moved to the forest, finding small scurrying creatures; birds; something hunting – he tensed for a moment, but the beast was not large, maybe a fox. It had found something much bigger than itself, and was hesitating, not certain whether to go closer: the thing might be meat, but if it was still alive . . . Through the fox's eyes Edmund could see only an indistinct shape in the gloom beneath the trees. Then the thing moved: the fox leapt back in alarm and ran away. But not before Edmund had seen a foot, wearing a stout leather boot.

'I've found him,' he said. 'This way.'

Their progress towards the trees was agonisingly slow at first. Their feet sank deep into the snow, and Edmund started to shiver uncontrollably. His blue cloak, given to him by the grateful king at Venta Bulgarum, had been meant for display, not warmth. He tried to put the cold aside and think only of Cathbar. The man was not dead (*not yet*, whispered a treacherous little voice). The man's eyelids flickered at times: if he concentrated, Edmund could see indistinct flashes of grey and white, and feel the life behind them. It was dangerous even to look, he knew. *Use the sight of one about to die*, he'd been warned, *and you lose your own sight, for ever*. But he kept slipping back, as if he could keep Cathbar alive by the force of his own will. 'He's unconscious,' was all he would tell Elspeth. 'We need to reach him quickly.'

The two of them spoke little after that, concentrating on keeping their footing. As they neared the forest the snow grew mercifully thinner and Edmund quickened his pace, driven as much by the cold as by his concern for Cathbar. The trees looked like a haven from the bleak expanse of snow – but it was no warmer beneath them, only darker. Elspeth's sword had faded, and they walked through a black-green gloom, punctuated with thin shafts of light and filled with the scent of pine needles. The world had shrunk to rows of rough trunks, carpeted with snow wherever the sky was visible above the branches. One opening, unusually large, let in slanting rays of sun. Two bushy branches dangled brokenly down – and beneath them was Cathbar.

To his relief, Edmund saw that the man's eyes were open, and he was breathing. He lay awkwardly, half-propped against a broad trunk and surrounded by the branches that he had brought down in his fall. As they approached he stiffened, tried to rise and slumped back, his eyes unfocused.

Elspeth ran to him. 'He's badly burned, Edmund. Help me!' She was already scooping handfuls of snow from the ground and laying them on Cathbar's face and shoulder. Edmund saw that the skin of the man's face was an angry red; his clothes blackened all down the right side. 'What should I do?' he asked, feeling suddenly stupid and helpless.

'Find some more snow – clean snow. I've seen tar burns on my father's ship; they're like this. You have to cool them!'

They worked steadily, laying on fresh snow as each handful melted, and the burned skin gradually lost its feverish heat, though it looked no better. When the slanting sunlight fell directly on his face, Cathbar groaned and opened his eyes.

'You found me, then,' he croaked. 'Good work. Burned up, am I?'

'It'll heal,' Elspeth told him. But her voice sounded uncertain, and looking at the man's ravaged face, Edmund wondered if she believed it.

'Cathbar,' he burst out, 'why did you follow us? We owe you more than we can ever repay, but this . . .'

'You owe me nothing, lad,' retorted Cathbar. They had to bend close to hear him, but his voice already had some of its old briskness. 'I was doing my duty, nothing more.' He looked around the little clearing, and shivered violently. 'Keeping you alive, and myself too,' he said. 'And if we're to keep alive much longer, I'd say we should be thinking about a fire, and maybe some shelter. Seems to me, we're in the Snowlands, and that's a bad place to be outside after dark.'

Elspeth nodded, and she and Edmund ran to gather sticks for a fire – but Edmund was suddenly uneasy. *A bad place to be outside after dark.* He remembered the wariness he had sensed in the fox's mind. Were there other hunters in this forest, larger than a fox? He said nothing, but began, cautiously, to feel around him for eyes.

As they began to lay a fire, Cathbar told Elspeth about a campaign he had been on in the Far North, and about some of the customs of the Snowlanders he had met. He was sitting up now, and seemed a little better: his voice was gaining strength, and Elspeth listened with the interest of the keen traveller. But Edmund was still casting his sight around, his wariness growing. There was something . . . Oh yes.

He was slinking low to the ground, senses wound up to a needle-point of alertness, the distant scent of meat sharpening the hunger in his belly. And on all sides were his companions, sleek and grey, younger and stronger than him, but not so fierce . . . not quite so hungry . . .

Edmund snapped himself back. 'We need to move,' he said urgently. 'Get out of the trees. There are creatures stalking us.'

Cathbar cursed and tried to haul himself up, subsiding with a groan. Edmund and Elspeth together managed to get him to his feet and he leant heavily on Edmund, breathing hard, his burns livid against the sudden pallor of his face.

'Just give me a moment to catch my breath,' he muttered. Still holding on to Edmund's arm, he took a step, winced and stood still until his breathing subsided before trying another. The next step seemed easier.

'I'll do well enough now,' he told them. 'My sword's over there, if you'll fetch it for me. And take the wood; we'll have need of it later.'

Elspeth led the way back out of the forest, following their footprints in the patches of snow and the shafts of sunlight, slanting now and growing paler. Cathbar and Edmund followed haltingly. Edmund wished they could go faster, but the captain's weight dragged at him: the man made no sound of complaint, but he was sweating despite the cold and his face was still pale. Edmund cast his sight back as often as he felt he could risk it, feeling his way over the uneven ground. The creatures behind them were spreading out, hoping to surround them before they left the trees. He felt their confidence as they tracked their slow, blundering prey: they were not even really hurrying. Only the hungriest one, the old male whose eyes he had borrowed first, was creeping closer than the rest, eager to get in early at the kill . . .

Edmund stumbled painfully on a root, his eyes snapping back to his own surroundings; he had been trying to break into a run, dragging Cathbar with him.

'I can see the snow ahead,' Elspeth called back to them.

Edmund felt the sweat break out on his face. But it was true: the trunks were thinning out ahead of them, and through the trees he could see sunlight, an expanse of snow, and in the distance, jagged grey mountains. Elspeth was almost there already.

Behind them, faintly at first, the wolves began to howl.

CHAPTER THREE

I was already an old man: how could I save the world? I make ploughs now, and cooking pots – not swords, I said. Let me stay with my wife and son: they'll have long enough without me. The Fay do not age, it's said, and my wife seemed no older to me than when she had left her people, though our boy was near eighteen. His light heart, and his mother's beauty, were all my joy. Was I to leave them? For the sword must be taken to the cold lands, my visitors told me. Without it, all would be lost.

Cluaran closed the door swiftly behind him. He had little time before the summoning, and no wish to be disturbed.

He raised his lantern and looked around the chamber with grim satisfaction. In the flickering yellow light it seemed larger than it was, extending into darkness at the back where the walls gave way to the bare rock of the hillside. The great iron frame with its straps of leather still stood there, but Orgrim, the man who had used it on his victims, lay now in prison, mad and blinded. Cluaran was not given to shuddering, but he turned his head and would not look at the thing again.

It was an evil place, Orgrim's hidden chamber under the hill. The king had declared it forbidden territory, but Cluaran was not of this kingdom; he went where he pleased. He turned to the shelf of books, scanning the spines in the light of the lantern. When he was last here, he had taken Orgrim's spell books, evidence for the king of his chief minister's treachery. But there was one other book here, one that Orgrim should never have seen; that *no one* else would see, now.

There it was: a thin cloth-bound volume, its cover stained the dull red of old blood. Cluaran opened the first page to look at the familiar words again. They rang in his mind in a voice long unheard, a voice he would never hear again however long he journeyed.

He snapped the book shut and stowed it deep in his pack. Now, at least, he had all he needed for the journey ahead.

The great hall of King Beotrich was full of old men in red. It was only two days since the King's Rede had been recalled, and Cluaran pictured the flurry across the kingdom as the faded robes were hastily recalled from the bottoms of chests, or from their four years' duty as blankets. The sons and brothers of the Redesmen executed by Orgrim had yet to return from exile, and old Aagard, by rights their leader, would still be journeying to the town from the far west – but still, the Rede had been restored.

Cluaran felt every eye on him as he entered the hall. He was the only beardless man present; to all appearances the youngest man in the room by far. He was certainly the drabbest, with his slight build and plain brown tunic, but the voices stilled as he made his bow to the throne, and the king looked deeply relieved to see him.

'Master Cluaran, you're welcome here,' Beotrich said quietly. Turning to the assembled thanes, he raised his voice: 'I here open the King's Rede, and I call on it for counsel.' The formal words sounded awkward, as well they might, Cluaran thought, after four years of neglect and misrule. But Beotrich went on more strongly, his eyes steady as he recalled his past folly.

'I declare before the Rede that I have been misled and deceived by the false counsellor Orgrim. The traitor is in prison, and those who were falsely accused by him are pardoned. I myself will pay the blood-price to the families of those who died, and their lands will be restored to their kin. But we now face a grave threat.' He gazed around the room, his anxiety evident on his face. 'The two children who revealed Orgrim's treachery to me have been taken, carried off by a monster, and my loyal captain Cathbar along with them: an evil reward for such faithfulness.' He was silent a moment, and when he went on his face was grim. 'I have no doubt that the creature was sent by Orgrim or whatever demon he serves, and designed to bring war on our kingdom. For the boy, Edmund, was the son of King Heored of Sussex.'

A murmur of shock and dismay swept the hall. 'But, my lord – it was none of your doing!' protested one greybeard. 'The boy was your honoured guest.'

Beotrich shook his head impatiently. 'For a few hours! And before that he was my prisoner. Heored is a hasty man – what will he think when he learns I had his son arrested? Or that he was dragged to his death from my own hall?'

'He's not dead.'

Cluaran's voice was as sharp as he could make it. These wittering fools! 'The one who sent the dragon wants his captives alive,' he said, in the shocked hush that followed. 'And, my lord, you have mistaken the danger you face. By the time Heored returns from his campaign, he and you, and every kingdom in this land, will be threatened by worse than dragons. And you must band together from this moment on, or die.'

The hall erupted into cries of outrage, scorn, even laughter. But Cluaran had spent half a lifetime dealing with unruly crowds. His voice slipped through the uproar like a knife blade.

'The crystal sword has returned! Many of you have seen it, and the Rede, of all people, know what that means. It was bound to return only at the time of greatest need: when the Chained One was about to break his chains. It is our only hope of protection against him – and now it's the source of our greatest danger.'

There was quiet now. Many of his hearers had gone pale. The old man who had spoken before ventured: 'But Orgrim is in prison. If the sword was freed by his meddling –'

'It was not,' Cluaran told him. 'He failed even to open the chest which held it. No, Orgrim was a distant and weak servant of our enemy. He has others, and stronger. How else do you think the dragon was unleashed again, with Orgrim crippled and blind?' Now that he had their attention he spoke lower, making the old men by the door lean forward to catch his words. 'The dragon has flown north to the Snowlands, where the Chained One lies. It is there that he was imprisoned, in the depths beneath his mountain – but he has learnt to reach beyond his prison, to bend others to his will again. It was he, or his servants, who sent the dragon – to bring him the girl, Elspeth, because she bears the sword. Oh, he wants Edmund for himself too; he thinks all Ripente belong to him, because their power is so much akin to his own. But the sword . . . the sword is the only thing on earth that can free him. If the girl is in his hands, we are lost.'

Now there was true silence, thick and heavy, while Cluaran looked a challenge at the king and every other man avoided his eye. At length Beotrich spoke.

'I'll give you an army,' he said. 'A hundred men. If you know where the dragon is taking the children, then follow it, and free them.'

There was murmuring among the Rede; one man called

out: 'Would you leave the kingdom undefended?' and others muttered agreement. But Cluaran was already on his feet.

'No need for the men,' he cried, almost light-hearted now that he had carried his point. 'Give me a letter of passage, a swift horse, and money for a boat. I'll be faster alone – and if I'm too late, a thousand men would make no difference.'

As the king shouted orders, Cluaran beckoned to the Redesman who had twice spoken before. 'Godric, you can help me if you will.' He turned and strode to the door, while the old man was still stumbling to his feet.

Outside, evening had fallen, and the square was lit by smoking torches to each side of the hall's great door. Cluaran shrugged off his pack and slipped into the shadows to one side. He waited to be sure Godric came out alone before stepping forward, and the old man, blinking about him in the dimness, started as Cluaran said his name.

'Godric, I know you as an honest man, and a friend of Aagard. You know he's returning?'

Godric's eyes brightened. 'It'll be a glad day when I see him again, master minstrel – for me and for all Wessex. He'll set things to rights.'

'I mean to help him do so,' Cluaran said. He reached into the pack and drew out a cloth-wrapped bundle. 'In here are Orgrim's spell books. I need not tell you how powerful they are . . . or how dangerous.' Indeed, the old man's face had turned white at the words, and he hesitated to touch the parcel.

'They must be kept under lock and key and no one but Aagard must see them,' Cluaran went on. '*No one.* He will know how to use them wisely.'

Godric took the bundle gingerly, as if it were a live creature that might bite him. With sudden resolution, he thrust it into the breast of his robe. 'I'm honoured by your trust, Master Cluaran,' he said. 'You're right: Aagard is wise enough to use such things – and I'm wise enough not to. No one will see them but him.' He took Cluaran's hand for a moment, then turned and hobbled off into the shadows.

Left alone, Cluaran leant against the brick-built wall, for all the world as though it were a tree in his own forest, not the house of a king. He could hear men running to saddle him the fastest horse in Beotrich's stables: before moonrise he would be on his way.

For the moment, though, no one paid him any heed. He delved in his pack once more and pulled out the slim book he had taken that day from the cave, running his hand over its spine almost in a caress. Its ox-blood cover was black in the torchlight; no other mark on it but a silver sword shape, gleaming in the smoky light. Cluaran opened it gently. He glanced around to be sure that he was alone, then looked at the first page.

'Here begins *The Book of the Sword . . .*'

CHAPTER FOUR

A sword made of all the substances of earth, they had said; *fire and ice; wood, metal and stone.* Though I complained, their words had lit a fire in me, and it grew as I worked.

But I could not make it sharp enough. Blade after blade snapped or warped, while I built the fire ever higher, sought out purer ores. I neglected other work, my family, even when we went hungry. One night I slept at the forge while the latest blade cooled, and woke with a vision in my head. I must take the sword to the Snowlands. I would find the help I needed there – from a girl.

There were a dozen wolves circling them, while more emerged from the trees. Looking at them through his own eyes, Edmund thought of his father's hunting dogs, surrounding a stag at bay. He had never liked watching the kill. And the grey-furred creatures closing in on them now were bigger than any hound kept at his father's palace.

The crystal sword burned white in Elspeth's hand, and the great beasts treated her warily, keeping their distance, with their haunches tucked under them. She whirled and stabbed as one of the wolves edged behind her and the creature leapt back, yowling, on three legs. But there were many more with four strong legs, and they ventured closer all the time. Cathbar was on his feet, slashing and lunging, but his blade was dulled from his attack on the dragon and his movements were uncertain; he had not so much as drawn blood. As for Edmund, he had no sword, only a short dagger, and the wolves seemed to be all around him. Already the boldest animals were snapping at his arms, their breath making a cloud about him in the icy air as he backed away. Their rank smell surrounded him on all sides.

The old male, the one whose eyes he had borrowed, lunged at Edmund's left side, its teeth clashing shut a hair's breadth from his thigh. He lunged in return, burying the dagger to the hilt in coarse grey fur. The wolf backed, but did not run howling. He'd barely wounded it! The blade in his hand was dark with blood, but the old wolf was not even slowed: it was coming at him again, and his answering strike was too slow. It took hold of his sleeve, the yellow eyes a hand's span from his own as it bunched its muscles to spring.

Something barged into Edmund, knocking him sprawling. Through a faceful of snow he saw the blaze of Elspeth's sword, and heard the old wolf's yelps. He pulled himself groggily to his feet. *Must she always protect me?* he thought – but there was no time for that now. He realised he had lost his knife; it lay in the snow several yards away, but before he could reach it a wolf bundled into his knees, making him stagger. Beside him, Elspeth spun in a ring of white fire, sending the wolves scrabbling frantically away in all directions. The one that had hit Edmund barely stopped to snap at him on its headlong dash towards the shelter of the trees. Next moment it had vanished into the wood, its tail down. The other wolves were still milling about the travellers, keeping a safe distance. Edmund tried to keep all of them in view at once as he edged towards his knife. But he froze again at a hoarse cry from Cathbar, his eyes following the man's outstretched arm. From the trees behind him, not far from where the fleeing animal had disappeared, another wolf stepped out, its breath pluming ahead of it as its jaws gaped wide.

It was huge. Its coat was darker than those of the other wolves, and from where he stood Edmund could see the play of muscles beneath as it stood looking at the three travellers. The other animals stopped their skittering and stood still, two dozen yellow eyes fixed on their leader as it made up its mind and turned unhurriedly towards Edmund.

I could dive for the knife, he thought. *Then I'll be on my belly in the snow when it springs. But there's nothing else I can do . . .* He began to run, his feet slipping in the powdery snow, just as the great beast leapt.

He felt it land on him as he got to the dagger: its claws raking his back; its hot breath on his neck. He staggered, trying to reach down for the knife with his right hand while his left flailed helplessly behind him. But no teeth ripped at him. The weight slid from his shoulders and he turned, dazed and still terrified, to see the wolf lying at his feet with an arrow in its back.

A young woman came striding out of the forest, the bow still in her hand. She seemed barely to notice Edmund as she crossed to the fallen wolf, slinging the bow over her back and drawing a long knife. In one graceful movement she knelt by the dying animal and cut its throat. Then she wiped her knife on the snow, jumped to her feet and stood for a moment over its body, nodding in satisfaction.

The wolf pack had fled. Besides their leader only one, the old scarred male, lay dead in the snow. The girl strode over to look at his scrawny body for a moment, then vanished into the trees and returned, dragging a rough wooden sled. She seemed a year or two older than Edmund, and a full head taller, dressed in leather leggings under a fur cape and hood. She nodded to him, and to the others who had come up behind him, her glance curious but not unfriendly. Then she turned, calling over her shoulder in a language he did not understand, and began to drag the body of the wolf she had killed to her sleigh. When Edmund made no move she paused and spoke again, impatient now.

'She says the old one is ours.' Elspeth had come up behind him, the sword fading in her hand. 'If we want him we need to take him away and skin him quickly, before the other wolves come back. It's the Dansk speech,' she explained, as he

36

looked at her in bewilderment. 'Most of the Northmen use it; I heard it often on trading voyages.'

Edmund was suddenly hot with shame: to need rescuing from a pack of animals, and by two girls! Elspeth had had no need to rush in and lose him his knife, as if he couldn't protect himself. But the Northern girl had truly saved his life and he couldn't even thank her. At the moment he could not tell which embarrassed him more.

The strange girl was still looking at him, her blue eyes curious. Then she took a step towards him and spoke, slowly and clearly, her voice surprisingly deep. '*Ek . . . heiti . . . Fritha. Ok thu?*'

'She says her name's . . .' Elspeth began, behind him.

'I could work that out for myself!' Edmund told her. He could feel his face burning, but he managed to look up at Fritha with something like a smile.

'Edmund,' he mumbled. 'And . . . thank you.'

She bobbed her head in acknowledgement and turned back to her work at the sleigh. Cathbar had come up, moving slowly. He had not been wounded by the wolf attack, but still seemed in great pain: half his face was burned dark red, and his blackened clothes clung ominously to his right side.

'Seems I was right, then,' he said. 'We're in the Snowlands right enough, and I can be of some help to you here.' His voice was beginning to slur. 'Soon as I've had . . . a bit of a . . .' His eyes rolled and, folding gently to his knees, he fell face forward in the snow.

Elspeth's cry of alarm brought Fritha running back over. She looked at Cathbar's shoulder and exclaimed in horror. Then she ran to tip the dead wolf off her sleigh and signalled Elspeth and Edmund to help her lay Cathbar there instead. She hefted the wolf's carcass over one shoulder as if it weighed no more than a cloak, and took up the leading-ropes of the sleigh.

'*Komm, nu!*' she told them urgently, and led the way into the forest.

Her name was Fritha Grufsdottir, she told them as they walked, taking turns to pull the sleigh. She lived in the forest with her father, who worked as a *kolmathr*, whatever that was. Edmund could understand a few of the words she used, and Elspeth would help with an occasional translation, though for most of the journey she was ranging around them watching for wolves, the crystal sword throwing a little patch of light about her. Fritha looked at the sword with open fascination, but without alarm, as far as Edmund could see. She was clearly curious about the strangers, but it was hard to explain anything to her while they were weaving their way through the endless trunks and dodging low branches; besides, his teeth were chattering with the cold. His arm knocked against a tree, tipping a load of snow down his neck, and he cursed silently. He was carrying the body of the scrawny old wolf, meaning to offer its skin to Fritha in thanks for her help, but it was unwieldy and kept slipping off his shoulder. The sleigh-rope cut into his hand, he ached all over, and he could not stop shivering. He looked at Fritha, striding so confidently through the trees, and Elspeth, intent on her watching, and wished that *he* were the one protecting the party, instead of following behind like a child.

The gloom of the forest gradually deepened until Fritha was only a vague shape in the darkness ahead, and keeping his footing took all of Edmund's attention. Elspeth, walking behind them, had allowed the sword to fade to a pale gleam, as if afraid of attracting unfriendly eyes. He thought he heard her stumble, and was wondering how much further they could manage to go, when Fritha gave a satisfied exclamation and led them out of the trees.

A sliver of moonlight showed a wide clearing, with stacks of wood piled at one end. A faintly glowing kiln stood a little way from the stacks, and at the other end of the clearing was a large hut, smoke rising from the centre of its pitched roof.

'*Fethr*!' Fritha called, dropping the sleigh-rope and running to the hut as a huge, fair-bearded man emerged from the doorway. The two of them talked briefly, and then the man pulled aside the skins hanging over the entrance and gestured to Edmund and Elspeth to go in.

'*Aufusa-gestra*,' he told them. The beard hid most of his expression, but the tone of his gravelly voice told Edmund that they were welcome.

He found himself standing a little straighter. He was light-headed with tiredness, and longed only to sit down – but this man was offering his roof and board to three strangers, appearing from nowhere. 'Thank you for your hospitality,' he said formally, and bowed his head before following the man inside.

Fritha's father, who introduced himself as Grufweld, gave up his bed to Cathbar, who was still unconscious, and Fritha tended his burns while the rest of them gathered around the fire in the centre of the hut. Later, Edmund remembered chiefly the glorious warmth, and how hard it was to keep awake as he sat with a bowl of meat stew in his hands, listening while Elspeth tried to tell their story. She spoke the Dansk tongue haltingly, with many gestures and lapses into English, but her listeners seemed to understand her. Edmund had not expected to be believed, but Grufweld listened gravely, while Fritha cried out in amazement to hear of the flight through the sky, Cathbar's battle with the dragon and their miraculously safe landing.

The hut was small for five people to sleep in, but Fritha laid down furs for Elspeth between her own bed and the fire, and made up a similar place for Edmund next to Cathbar. Grufweld, it seemed, would stay up all night. The last thing Edmund remembered was the sight of the big man, hunched on a wooden stool over the low-banked fire, while the wind keened outside the hut and Cathbar muttered and groaned beside him in his sleep.

Light pressed against Edmund's eyelids, and he blinked and pulled himself up, looking around in confusion for a moment until the memory came back. The hut looked even smaller by daylight; only a dozen paces from end to end, its floor covered unevenly with hides, but with no furniture other than a couple of wooden chests and the pallets they lay on. A shaft of bright sunlight came through the doorway, where the hanging skins had been tied back. The fire still burned low, but apart from himself and Elspeth, the hut was empty.

Elspeth cried out in her sleep. Edmund climbed off his pile of furs, wincing – every muscle in his body seemed to ache – and went over to her. At the touch of his hand on her shoulder she woke with a start, looking up at him with wide eyes.

'It hates me so much – I can't bear it . . .' Her voice was choked.

'Elspeth, you're dreaming! What hates you?'

She focused on his face, and her own gradually relaxed.

'I can't tell . . . Something in the fire . . . It was all burning, Edmund, and there was a man falling . . . and Cluaran was there! But why would he . . . ?' She looked bewildered for a moment; then, with a visible effort, sat up and shook her head as if to clear it.

'You're right,' she said. 'It was just a dream.' She clambered to her feet. 'Look, Edmund, Cathbar's bed is empty. He must be feeling better!'

They pulled on their shoes and hurried to the door. The cold air was like knives on Edmund's skin, and freshly fallen snow lay all around the hut, though an area had been cleared just outside it and laid with straw mats. Cathbar was sitting beside the doorway on a seat made from a slice of tree trunk, sharpening his sword on a stone. Fritha had cut away his burned clothing the night before, and he now wore a heavy fur cloak, fastened at the neck, but his right arm, coated with thick green salve, was bared to the frosty air as he worked. The captain seemed not to notice. He moved his arm stiffly, but his back was straight, and he looked up at Edmund and Elspeth with a crooked smile. His face was puckered and scarred, but already less livid in colour than it had been the day before.

'On my feet again, as you see,' he said. 'That young maid has a rare skill with her salves! Must be on account of her father's work.' He gestured towards the other end of the clearing, where Grufweld was bent over the kiln. 'Charcoal-burner,' he explained. 'I warrant he's had some bad scalds in his time.'

Grufweld straightened up as he spoke, and called to them in his deep voice, gesturing towards the hut. 'He says you'd be better off inside, dressed like that!' Cathbar translated. 'His girl plans to make us all some warmer gear. And he says if we'll stop with him three or four days more his charcoal will be ready for market, and we can go along with him to the nearest village. We'll make our way to the coast from there and take ship back home.'

'We can't do that!' Elspeth burst out.

Edmund nodded vehemently. Grufweld had given up his bed for them last night; had made supper for five when he had food for two. How could they stay with him for another three days?

'Hard to know what else we can do,' Cathbar was saying. 'He told me the village is two days' walk away, and there's no road.'

'Please tell him,' Edmund said, 'that we're more grateful than we can say for his help, but it would abuse his hospitality to stay so long. I think I can find our way.' He had already cast his sight into the dark trees all around, looking for eyes, and found nothing but a bird or two. 'I'll be able to tell when we're near a village,' he added.

Cathbar shrugged, heaved himself to his feet and trudged through the snow to talk to Grufweld, who had turned back to his work. Elspeth took Edmund's arm, and he saw a sudden urgency in her face.

'Edmund,' she said awkwardly, 'you and Cathbar should go to the village, but I don't think I can. There's somewhere else I need to go.'

'What do you mean?' Shock made Edmund's voice shrill. 'On your own? Go where?'

'I don't know yet.' Elspeth's voice was steady, but she avoided his eyes, looking down instead at her right hand. 'But I think I'll find out very soon.'

He was about to protest, but at that moment Fritha appeared from behind the hut with a long knife in her hand and streaks of blood on her bare arms. She walked lightly, her fair plaits swinging, and Edmund noticed that her wide-soled boots stopped her feet from sinking into the snow as his did.

'*Al-gerr!*' she called to her father. Seeing Edmund and Elspeth, she flashed them a smile and said something else.

'She's thanking us for the wolfskin,' Elspeth explained, when he looked helplessly at her. Fritha nodded.

'*Ja*,' she said, and added, carefully, 'Thenk . . . for vulf.'

She took them to see the two new skins hanging in the tiny, reeking drying-shed behind the hut, and showed them the already cured skins that she had cut out to make leggings for her unexpected guests. Edmund was ashamed to think of the work they were giving her, but when he tried to protest she replied firmly, through Elspeth, that she could not let a guest die of cold!

'But she says we can help her,' Elspeth added, and Fritha set all three of them up on tree-stump seats outside the hut, draped in furs for warmth, sewing with bone needles. Edmund had never done such work before, and had to keep stopping to blow on his numb fingers, or unpick clumsy stitches. Fritha and Elspeth talked as they worked, and Edmund found that he could pick up much of what Fritha said. She would not hear of them leaving her father's home alone; Grufweld would need to watch the kiln for some days yet, but if they were determined to leave now, she would go with them. It was too dangerous for strangers to be in the forest on their own.

'We can deal with wolves,' Elspeth said stoutly, but Fritha shook her head, her blue eyes serious. It was not only wolves that they had to fear.

'There are *vakar* . . . holes in the ice. Very dangerous. And there . . .' she pointed towards the east, '*Eigg Loki*.'

Edmund heard Elspeth gasp. Fritha started to describe the terrible fire-mountain that once spewed flame and molten rock over the land; now it was the home of spirits that could entice you into its crevasses . . .

But Edmund knew what was coming. A faint, pulsing glow had begun to shine from Elspeth's hand as soon as the mountain was named. Elspeth dropped her needle, and stared towards the east as if listening to another voice than Fritha's.

'That's where I must go,' she whispered.

CHAPTER FIVE

It grieved me sorely to go. I had travelled far enough in my life already. With a sad heart I said farewell to my wife and son, certain I would never return. But my boy, my chattering Starling, was afire to come with me.

– There's nothing there but ice, and wolves, and death from cold! I told him.

But he would not be moved. And at length I weakened, and my wife too.

– Go, she said, and we'll both come with you.

'That sword has turned you addled, girl! There's no question of it. You're going straight back home, the two of you.'

Cathbar's face was red, the burn marks showing painfully dark, but his voice was stronger than Elspeth had heard it since leaving Venta Bulgarum. They were all standing in a huddle outside Grufweld's hut: Cathbar had leapt to his feet in outrage as soon as he heard her plans, and refused to sit down though it was clear his legs were none too steady. She tried again to explain that she could not go back; that the mountain was where she needed to be, but the captain was not listening.

'I came here to bring you back safe. Do you think I'll let you go journeying over the ice? Among the wolves? To a fiery mountain?' He jabbed a finger at her as he spoke, his hand shaking. Edmund, his face tight with concern, took him by the arm, but said nothing. Fritha looked on uncomprehendingly, clearly unhappy at the argument.

'I'm sorry,' Elspeth said again. She could feel the sword's energy throbbing in her arm, and its voice rang in her head, as familiar to her as her own voice, but sweeter, more powerful. 'The sword would have brought me here, even without the dragon. I have to take it to *Eigg Loki*.'

'But how can you tell?' Edmund cried. 'We never even heard the name before. How can you suddenly *know* that you need to go there?'

Elspeth fought for words. How could she explain the certainty that had filled her, coursing like a storm-wave through her whole body? 'The sword told me,' she said.

Edmund and Cathbar started to talk at once. Grufweld's deep voice cut through theirs; the big man had come up behind them unheard, rolling a section of tree trunk through the snow.

'I think,' he said in Dansk, 'it is time for us to eat.' He gestured for Cathbar to sit on the piece of wood. 'And after food you will work out your dispute. Fritha, fetch the barley loaf.'

The charcoal-burner looked very grave when Elspeth explained to him where she must go, and Fritha turned pale. They sat outside the doorway of the hut, in the brief warmth of the midday sun. Out of courtesy to their hosts, they had not spoken until the bread was eaten, and Cathbar had had time to regain a measure of calm.

Elspeth had eaten without tasting the food, her mind running over what she was to say. It was so hard to explain to them all how she knew what she must do. The sword was pulling her; that was true: she could feel its voice, its will, even now, tugging at her thoughts. But there was more than that. The sword was a part of her now, and it was hard to untangle its ends from her own. *After all, what do I have to go back for?* she asked herself. *I believe that the sword has a destiny: some good that it can do at* Eigg Loki. *And what better purpose can I have than to take it there?* She tried to put her conviction into words, as Cathbar scowled and Grufweld shook his head.

'*Eigg Loki* is a bad place,' the big man said gravely. 'You should not go there – it would be better if no one did. You have heard of Loki?'

Yes! hissed the sword's voice, but Elspeth needed no reminding. The name had been at the back of her mind ever since Cluaran had used it on the hillside outside Orgrim's cave, warning her that the evil she had fought was not yet defeated. *He tried to destroy all that the gods had created . . . Loki, the wily one.*

'He is a god – or a demon,' she said. 'He was chained up beneath a mountain. And is *Eigg Loki . . . ?*'

48

Grufweld nodded. 'It was a hundred years ago and more, but the stories are still told: how he nearly escaped from the chains the gods had made, and burned the land; and an army died to bind him again. Some say he still lives under the mountain, and the spirits of the rocks and water are his servants.' He paused, and when he spoke again his voice was gruffer. 'I can't say if the stories are true, but I fear the spirits that live below the mountain. They took my wife, Fritha's mother.' He fell silent again, his head lowered. Fritha, beside him, put her hand on his shoulder.

'I was eight,' she told them softly. 'It was summer; my father was fishing in the lake below *Eigg Loki*, and we went to gather cloudberries on the lake shore. But my mother said she heard voices and went in search of them. They drew her on to the ice at the far edge of the lake, and when I called after her she did not hear me – until the ice broke.'

Soul-eaters! cried the sword in Elspeth's mind. *How much longer will they do Loki's work? Let me stop him!*

The force of the words pulled Elspeth to her feet. Her right arm throbbed fiercely, and she saw that it had begun to glow. She held it in her other hand, looking down at the startled faces around her.

'What did you say, girl?' Grufweld's voice was suddenly harsh. 'What do you know about the soul-eaters?'

'I don't . . .' she started to say, but was stopped by a shooting pain in her hand. The sword burst into life, its white brilliance dimming the pale sunlight. Fritha cried out in wonder.

'It's the sword that knows,' Elspeth said simply. 'It was made for this.'

'And if the dragon that brought us here was *sent* by this demon?' Cathbar burst out. 'What then? How do you know he's not waiting for you to come to him?'

Edmund was watching her intently, Elspeth saw. She avoided his eyes, looking full at Cathbar.

'If that's so, then he wanted us killed, or brought to him helpless. But I'm not helpless now! Cathbar – I know there's danger. But you've seen some of the sword's power: it will guide me, and it'll protect me on the journey. You go back with Edmund. I can travel alone, but I must go to *Eigg Loki*.'

Grufweld stared at her in silence for a long time. At last he turned to Cathbar, his face solemn. 'You are her guardian, not I,' he said. 'But I believe the child must do as she says.'

Cathbar said not a word. Grufweld rose and turned back to his kiln, summoning Fritha to help him. The sword blazed until it filled Elspeth's vision, calling her to start the journey now – now! But a hand laid on her arm called her back to herself. Edmund was standing beside her, his face filled with concern. 'You're certain of this?' he asked. 'You have to go there?'

'Never more certain,' she told him. 'I'm sorry to leave you, Edmund, but the sword will keep me safe. I know it will.'

'I'm not leaving you,' he said abruptly. 'We've come this far together. I'll go with you to the mountain. And if you really think you can defeat Loki, I'll help you.' She must have looked doubtful, for his grip on her arm tightened and he went on almost angrily. 'He destroyed my uncle! Whatever Aelfred . . . Orgrim did, he was still my kin. My mother would want him avenged.'

Behind them, Cathbar heaved himself noisily to his feet. 'Then there's no help for it,' the man grunted. 'The two of you seem intent on seeking out every foolishness and every danger, but I came here to protect you, and that job's not likely to be done for a while. I'll finish sharpening my sword.'

He lumbered inside the hut, where he had laid the grind-stone. Elspeth looked back at the crystal sword in her hand, its light dimming now. Edmund was saying something else to her, but all she could hear was the echo of the sword's voice in her head: *Let me stop him*. She gazed across the clearing, try-ing vainly to catch a glimpse of *Eigg Loki* above the forest. How long would it take to reach the mountain?

Over by the kiln, Fritha seemed to be in heated discussion with her father. Her voice, low but fervent, floated across to them, though Elspeth could not hear what she said. Eventually Grufweld nodded, and Fritha walked back to where Elspeth and Edmund stood.

'Elspeth,' she said, 'we have been talking, my father and I. We think it is not safe for you to go so far alone, or even with your companions. We know the country around *Eigg Loki* as you do not – we know where the dangers are. Even a sword will not protect you from the ice.' She glanced at Elspeth's right hand. The sword had vanished now, but her hand and arm were still touched with its radiance; Fritha looked at them almost with awe. 'My father has given me permission to come with you,' she said. 'I will be your guide to the fire-mountain.'

They left the following morning. Edmund had been baffled as he watched Elspeth prepare for the journey: she had argued so strongly that she must go, but now that they were getting ready to leave, she seemed strangely indifferent. She had listened to all Grufweld's warnings of the dangers ahead without any signs of excitement or fear, though Edmund had felt both, and had seen them on Fritha's face too. Even Cathbar had talked to the charcoal-burner at length, asking questions about the route and the terrain. Edmund had been full of relief when Fritha announced that she would accompany them, but Elspeth had only thanked the girl politely, as if she cared little whether they had help or not.

They were dressed now in the same clothes that Fritha and her father wore: leggings, wide fur boots, fur caps and rough capes that Fritha called *hafnar-feldr*, made of wolf fur. For the first time since his landing in the Snowlands, Edmund found he could walk in the snow without stumbling or shivering, the wide soles supporting his weight on the surface and the thick furs keeping out the chill. Grufweld had supplied them handsomely with food and blankets for the journey, and had spent some time that morning talking earnestly to Fritha, no doubt giving her more advice. Edmund had understood enough of the talk yesterday to know that she was returning to the place where she had lost her mother, and he felt a little awed at the girl's bravery in coming with them – and at Grufweld's sacrifice in letting her go. Fritha was plainly afraid of the mountain she called *Eigg Loki*, but Edmund thought he saw a light in her eyes when she talked of the journey: a sense of adventure, or maybe just curiosity. As they looked back at the charcoal-burner standing at the edge of his clearing, his hand raised in farewell, Edmund remembered his own mother, sending him away when danger threatened their home, and he vowed that he would do all he could to return Fritha safely to her father.

'Well, he's a sensible man, I'll say that for him,' Cathbar remarked as they turned away to the trees. 'Even if he's too easily impressed by omens and suchlike. Gave me some good tips for keeping out of trouble – and that girl of his seems to have a wise head on her shoulders.'

Cathbar was walking more easily today, though still slowly. As they followed Fritha and Elspeth through the trees he sometimes had to rest on Edmund for support when the ground became uneven, but he plainly hated to show this sign of weakness, and neither of them referred to it.

'Did Grufweld say anything about the sword?' Edmund asked as they negotiated a difficult clump of roots.

'He didn't seem as surprised by it as I'd have thought,' Cathbar admitted. 'Wanted to know how Elspeth came by it, and could I swear it was no evil enchantment. I told him the girl had the sword from a man I'd trust with my life, and as for evil enchanters – I saw one she'd struck down with it. And he said, "The gods speed you, then".' He gave a short laugh. 'And I hope they do, boy – and speed us back, more to the point.'

At first Fritha led them swiftly and confidently, but as the trees began to thin, showing occasional glimpses of the snow plains ahead, her pace slowed. Elspeth kept ceaseless watch about them, the sword flaring in her hand and growing brighter as the light began to fade. Edmund had begun to scan the forest for eyes, but so far nothing had seemed to threaten them: there were furry scurrying things not much bigger than a mouse, and a few woodland birds; nothing more. Yet Fritha seemed more and more anxious.

'We are near to the ice now,' she told them. 'When we come out of the trees, there are crevasses covered in powdered snow – *Úminni-gjar*.'

'Forgetting-places,' Cathbar translated. 'If you fall down one, you are lost for ever.'

It was nearly dusk when they reached the edge of the trees. The trunks became wider spaced, letting in shafts of reddish light, until suddenly they gave way altogether and there was nothing but emptiness ahead: an endless stretch of white, featureless apart from the red glints picking out hummocks in the snow. To their left, the trees stretched out northwards in a black line, while far off in the distance, indistinct grey mountains merged with the low, pink-streaked clouds. Elspeth was about to stride ahead on to the snow, but Fritha held her back.

'We must go northwards, follow the trees,' she said. '*Eigg*

54

Loki is north-east of here and we can shelter in the forest tonight.'

Elspeth made a small noise of frustration, but turned to walk along the line of trees, though Edmund saw her casting eager glances across the white wastes of snow towards the mountains. For himself, Edmund was happy to keep to the trees. The snow fields were so vast, so completely barren of life or shelter. He cast his sight out again – and stopped. There, in the trees behind him, was a flash of something that he recognised: low to the ground, but not a mouse or fox . . . panting . . . and the flash of a furred side.

'Wolves!' he cried.

The others stopped, Cathbar drawing his sword and Fritha fitting an arrow to her bow. But nothing came out of the trees towards them.

'You're sure?' Cathbar asked after a pause.

Edmund nodded. He could feel the wolves coming closer. For a moment he risked sharing the eyes of one of the animals: running with its mates, white-furred; intent on the quarry, but keeping a careful distance away . . . But this was different from before. The wolf was not hungry: it simply felt . . . watchful.

'Edmund!' Elspeth's voice disturbed him. 'Can't you find out what they're doing? We have to get on!'

Edmund bristled. 'They're not planning to attack us – not this moment, anyway,' he said stiffly. 'But they're very close. I think they're following us.'

They moved onwards, slowly and cautiously now. Fritha fell back to walk beside Edmund. '*Thu hefir andar-auga*?' she asked him. 'You have far-seeing?' When he nodded, she opened her blue eyes very wide. 'I never met one before,' she told him, with a new respect in her voice.

Edmund watched Fritha pick up her pace to take the lead again. He hoped she would not come to mistrust him because of his gift, as so many people did at home. Her opinion mattered to him, though he could not say why.

The line of trees led them in a sweeping curve towards the north-east. As the last of the light was fading, turning the snow fields to a vast, vague greyness and the trees to a solid black mass, Fritha stopped.

'We are nearly at the end of the woods,' she told them. 'We can go back into the trees to sleep – if it's safe, Edmund?'

Edmund cautiously sent his sight back to the wolves. They were still behind them, watching – but there was no sense of ferocity; no hunger. So what was it he could sense behind those yellow eyes? Something like interest – if they had been human, he might have said, concern.

Could the wolves be *guarding* them?

CHAPTER SIX

I will not speak much of the voyage. Storms followed us as if the Evil One had sent them to stop us, and my wife near pined away from the loss of her green trees and heathland. Only Starling kept up his spirits, and ours with them. And so we arrived, on a day of lowering clouds, at a land where it seemed nothing grew but ice, and rocks, and black pines.

Cluaran peered impatiently into the mist. There was no time to waste and the little craft was so slow! The sea crossing had been brisk enough: the sleek lines for which he had chosen the boat let her cut through the water smoothly when there was wind for the sail. But as soon as land loomed on the horizon, the wind had dropped almost to nothing; all the helmsman's skill could hardly move them. Cluaran had taken his turn at the oars with the other men at first as if his wiry strength could move the boat faster. But when the fog came down, the boat master had made him leave off. The sailors were looking askance at him, and the man nearest him had shifted as if to avoid touching him. Even before this bad luck they had mistrusted the passenger who had dragged them so far from their accustomed trading routes, no matter if he did pay in gold. Now, surrounded by white emptiness, they had begun to mutter of sorcery and the evil eye.

So Cluaran sat moodily in the stern, willing the land to come closer. He even thought of speaking to the wind, though he knew well that he only had a shadow of the true skill for it. But the ones who had power here would guide the boat, if they wished to see him. Though if they did, Cluaran knew, it would not be for anything good.

A sudden flare showed in the whiteness over the prow as the helmsman struck sparks from his fire-stone. He set light to a wad of cloth wound around an arrow and fired it into the fog. The little arc of flame showed bravely for a moment, then faded to nothing. But as the men began to groan the helmsman fitted a second burning arrow and fired again. There was no sound, but this time the arrow hit something. The little flare stopped in mid-air, hovering at mast-height, as the master changed course and the sailors cheered and slapped each other on the back in relief. Cluaran's relief was the equal of theirs, though he kept his face carefully neutral. Whatever the dangers ahead, he would be moving towards his goal again.

The fog began to clear, revealing tall black cliffs blotched with lichen – the spent arrow hung from a crevice – and the port beyond them. It was a tiny fishing village, little more than half-a-dozen huts facing on to an ice-covered beach and backed by dense forest. The sailors, their sullenness forgotten, pulled on the oars and the boat was soon entering the harbour – if you could give that name to three feet of wall built against a rock, Cluaran thought. It was set with a few ropes tied to hooks, and led to a low spur of the cliff, as grey with ice as the beach.

Cluaran checked that all was safely stowed in his pack, the book carefully wrapped in his oilskin. He stood up, balancing easily on the swaying boards, and leapt out as the helmsman brought the boat alongside the wall. The stone was slick with ice, but he had judged the jump well.

'No need to tie her, boat master!' he called. 'I'll say farewell, and you can catch the tide.'

The master was as keen as any of his men to leave this desolate place, but he must have felt some lingering sense of responsibility to his free-handed passenger. 'There's no one to meet you, master?' he asked doubtfully.

'I'm well known in the village,' Cluaran lied. 'They'll give me hospitality.'

The sailors cheered as the boat was turned around. Some of them, forgetting all about the evil eye, turned to wave at him as the gathering breeze caught the sail and sent them back to the safety of the trade route.

Cluaran made his way along the rocky causeway, his booted feet slipping with every step. He had lost maybe half a day in the calm; night fell quickly this far to the north, and he had far to go before dark. At the cliff face a flight of steps, hacked out of the rock, led down to the beach, and in his haste he stumbled on the last one, staggering for a pace or two on the icy pebbles before he recovered himself. In that unbalanced instant, a man stepped from an angle of the cliff and laid a knife to his throat.

'You should not have come,' said a quick, light voice in his ear.

Cluaran relaxed slightly. 'Ari. Well met to you too.'

The blade did not move. 'You know they have not forgiven you.'

'And I have never stopped loving her,' Cluaran said softly. The man did not move, and after a moment Cluaran reached up to lower the blade with his hand. He turned to look at Ari's face: pale as a candle, with eyes as green and cold as water seen through the ice. 'You haven't changed,' he said.

Ari's face was expressionless. 'No. But you have.'

Cluaran started to walk up the beach. 'Are you here to capture me, or help me? You know why I have come: the sword has returned, and its bearer is taken. For all I know, it's already at *Eigg Loki*.'

'No – not yet,' Ari told him, with more animation than he had shown before. 'There are still some of us who remember the old danger: we keep a watch on the mountain, and on any who go there. The dragon was seen in the sky three days ago: first flying towards the sea, then returning with captives in its claws. It let them fall in the snow fields – but we found no bodies, and two sets of prints leading into the trees. The

60

children are alive, and safe for now. But there are eyes on them. They may be walking into the very danger we fear.'

Cluaran had unconsciously quickened his stride. 'We must find them, then!' The other man was silent, and Cluaran turned to him impatiently. 'You'll come with me?'

'Yes . . .' Ari still hesitated. 'But first *you* must come with *me*. They want to see you.'

'At such a time!' Cluaran exploded.

Ari's face did not change, but he took Cluaran's arm with a slender hand. 'At any time,' he said firmly. 'There's a debt that must be paid. And then I'll help you.'

Cluaran bit back his protest. 'Oh, very well,' he said with bad grace. 'But we leave now, and walk all night, understand? It's a good three leagues further than I'd planned, and a vile crossing over ice and stone for most of it. I'd meant to keep to the trees, at least.'

Ari seemed surprised. 'But there's no need to go on foot!'

They had left the beach as he spoke, and were walking up a snow-covered track past the first of the huts. No one stirred inside, but behind the building, tied to a post, were two horses, stamping restlessly in the cold.

Even in his anxiety, Cluaran smiled. 'I'm in your debt, Master Ari,' he said. 'If I must run to meet trouble, what better way than on four legs?'

In another place, deep under the rock, the dragon brooded.

It had never failed before: never been wounded; never

loosed its prey. Now one of its eyes was darkened, and its fore-leg stiffened as it healed, lying at the wrong angle. Every time it moved, it gave a low rumble of pain and fury.

The mind behind its eyes had been angry, nearly angry enough to kill. The dragon felt again the volcano erupting in its head, screaming its rage, spewing molten fire over the whole world until nothing was left, nothing but charred stone and white ash . . . and then that fury had passed, and a cooler voice had whispered that the prey were not lost: they were still down there in the open, both of them, still moving. And if they could not be carried to the place, why, maybe they could be herded there.

Once, the dragon would not have done this. Once, it lived only for the sky and the chase: the swoop on the squeaking prey; the joy of skewering and rending; the rich taste of blood. But since the voices had entered its head, those days were past. Its mind was not capable of regret, but for an instant it formed a picture of plummeting down on the prey that had turned on it, biting into bits the shining spike that had hurt its leg and eye, and feasting . . .

It gave a long roar of remembered pleasure, the flame play-ing over the rock wall. Then, in obedience to the voices, it heaved itself up to the cave mouth, growling with pain, spread its great wings and leapt into the evening sky. Over the snow plain it soared in wide circles, one foreleg trailing, searching by scent, by the hunter's instinct and its one good eye, for the tiny creatures that it must not kill . . . not yet.

CHAPTER SEVEN

The fishermen at the harbour feared strangers and would give us no hospitality, but we had sent word ahead to a name that the Fay visitors left me – Erlingr. We sheltered that night in a cave, and were met there by Erlingr's men next morning.

They were pale as the ice, and kept back from our fire as if it would melt them. With them was a woman, barely more than a girl. She was pale in the face as they were, but her hair and eyes were black as coal. She looked on us with eagerness, as if we brought something she had long hoped to see. And my boy Starling looked at her in the same way.

They were close enough to the edge of the forest to catch slim fingers of the early morning sun. Each one touched Elspeth with new warmth, and she looked up at the pale blue sky between the trees with a rush of exhilaration. The excitement had been growing in her ever since they had set off at first light this morning: the others had grumbled about their damp blankets and stiff limbs, but Elspeth had hardly noticed them. She was on the right path; she knew it. She felt the weight of the invisible sword in her hand; she could conjure it so vividly in her mind that as she swung it, her eyes caught glints of sunlight as if reflected from the blade. And at the edge of hearing she could hear its voice – *her* voice, as familiar now to Elspeth as her own – murmuring that she must go on; go quickly. The sense of urgency was always with her, though she was still not sure what she would find in the mountains. Could there really be spirits in the rocks, as Fritha feared?

Elspeth shivered: a few days ago she had thought dragons were fables. She knew better now. The monster that had carried her off had flown towards *Eigg Loki*: would she have to fight it there? And what of Loki, the demon-god of Cluaran's story – and Grufweld's? Was he waiting for her in the depths of the mountain? Or was it just some evil influence, that called up dragons and sent men mad?

The cool voice in her head gave no answer. She whispered only, *Whatever dangers you face, I face with you.*

The voices of Elspeth's companions broke into her thoughts. Fritha was telling Edmund and Cathbar about her homeland: the darkness in the dead of winter when she and her father kept fires lit outside the hut night and day to scare off the wolves; the lakes in the shadow of the mountains where the fishermen camped until their catches were big enough to take back to the villages . . . and the mountains themselves, where no one ventured for fear of the beings that lived there.

Elspeth could understand the older girl fairly well, having heard the Dansk tongue often from the blond, bearded sailors who had traded with her father on voyages to Hibernia. Cathbar seemed to speak the language like a native, but Edmund was clearly having difficulties. Every sentence or so, he would stop Fritha to ask for explanations, then carefully translate her words with an English phrase which she, as carefully, repeated back to him. Through all her preoccupation, Elspeth could not keep back a smile to see them so earnest together. Edmund seemed taken with the Northern girl, she thought: his eyes were bright as he listened to her, and his pale face had more colour than Elspeth had seen since they came to this icy land. It warmed her to see Edmund's animation, but she could not share in the talk for now. Her mind was too full of the journey, and the thought of what might lie at the end of it.

They emerged from the last of the trees into a world of whiteness, lit with pink and gold by the low sun. Through the dazzle Elspeth could just make out the grey mass of the mountains to the north and east, their flanks white with freshly fallen snow. In every other direction the land stretched blue-white and level as far as the eye could see. She heard Edmund and Cathbar behind her, exclaiming in wonder. But Elspeth had eyes only for the mountains, and the golden light that lay on the snow like a path towards them: *the way I must go*.

She had started eagerly forward when Fritha pushed in front of her. '*Stothva-sik her!*' the older girl cried. 'Don't go too fast here! There is danger – the ice is close here, and beneath it is water . . . and the creatures that live in the water.'

'Fish, you mean?' Cathbar said hopefully. 'We'll need more food soon.'

'Worse things than fish,' Fritha told him. Her face was anxious. 'You must follow where I walk now – and tread carefully.'

Edmund fell in behind her at once, placing Cathbar ahead of him. The captain seemed fresher this morning, but his face was still an angry red all down one side, and his movements were slow and stiff. Elspeth, forced to take up the rear, felt a fierce impatience with their cautious pace: she could almost have wished she was travelling alone.

They trudged through the white wasteland in single file, following Fritha. The sun rose above the tallest peaks, driving away the blue shadows until the snow was dazzling white on all sides. There was no talk now, only the crunch of their boots in the snow. Elspeth kept her gaze fixed on the mountains, willing them to come closer, but their progress seemed maddeningly slow. Once, as Fritha stopped to test the ground, she glanced behind her: the trees were a dark smudge in the distance, and the snow stretched all around, broken only by the wavering line of their footprints. The size and emptiness of it dizzied her, and she turned quickly back to the others.

The mountains had grown closer; they stretched out now like arms to each side of the travellers. Fritha had turned northwards, heading for the centre of the range. Elspeth stared at the jagged peaks, wondering if she would somehow recognise her destination when she saw it. The sword had fallen silent, but before she could try to raise the voice in her head she was startled by a cry from Edmund.

'Look! There's smoke!'

Fritha nodded. '*Fiskimathar* – fish-mans,' she told him. They were near the mountain lakes, she explained, long, narrow run-offs from the glaciers, covered in ice now. Some of the bolder fishermen came here throughout the winter, melting holes in the ice with fire-pans to reach their catch.

'I thought there'd be fishing here!' Cathbar exclaimed. 'Are they hospitable, these men?'

Fritha looked grave. They were not bad men, she said; but they would be suspicious of strangers, especially in this place. She agreed to stop by the lake and make camp, but Elspeth could tell that she was nervous, whether of the men or of the place she could not tell.

The fishermen's camps soon appeared: a cluster of orange sparks which became smoky fires, and an uneven row of makeshift hide tents with tiny figures moving between them. The lake itself was mostly covered with snow, but near where the tents were thickest Elspeth could see great dark patches beneath the whiteness. Fritha saw them too: the fair-haired girl stood very still for a moment before she moved them on again. She walked slower now, treading lightly and prodding the ground ahead of her with a long branch. Finally she stopped, a good way away from the closest tents. The sun was dipping low in the sky behind them, and the blue-grey mountains reared around them on all sides.

'We have reached the lake,' Fritha told them. She used her branch to sweep away snow from the ground in front of them, uncovering a surface of dully gleaming ice. 'We'll camp here, and if we can break the ice, we can fish.'

They gratefully dropped their packs and firewood bundles. Cathbar showed Edmund how to scoop a hollow in the snow at the lake's edge and line it with thick branches before laying out charcoal for a fire, while Elspeth helped Fritha to peg together a set of short wooden rods from her pack as tent poles. Ahead of them, the evening sun struck glints from the ice and lit the upper slopes of the mountains. One peak stood out above the others. What looked like a river of ice ran down it to one side, glowing in the yellow light and making the rocks around it look black in comparison. Elspeth felt her hand throb. *There!* came the voice in her head.

'Is that *Eigg Loki*?' she asked.

Fritha nodded. 'You can see the glacier running down it to the lake.' To Elspeth's surprise she started to hum. 'It's a song my mother sang to me when I was little,' she explained. 'It says, *Ice spirits in the glacier, water spirits in the lake; cold brothers.* It didn't make me scared then because the tune was so

68

sweet. But since my mother died, I don't like it so much.' She turned abruptly to the packs and started shaking out blankets to drape over the tent poles. Elspeth felt a sudden longing to go to the older girl and take her hand, to tell her about her own father, drowned so short a time before. But she felt awkward, and busied herself instead in helping Fritha with the tent.

They joined Cathbar and Edmund around the small fire, and ate some of their dwindling supply of bread and dried meat. Elspeth realised for the first time how hungry she was and thought longingly of fresh fish – but Fritha explained that they could not melt the ice as the fishermen did: the men did not light fires on the ice itself, but used hot charcoal in a metal pan with a long handle, which she did not own. They could try to fish if they liked, for tomorrow's meal, but they would have to break the ice with knives, if they could. After the scanty dinner, Fritha found a spot where she thought the ice was thinnest, and Edmund gladly began to chip at it with his knife. But after a dozen blows, he looked up in frustration.

'I've barely scratched it!' he complained, looking ruefully at the pitted surface. 'Elspeth, couldn't the sword help us?'

Elspeth started towards him, but something held her back. She felt – what was it? A strange sense of reluctance, almost fear. Why shouldn't she use the sword? She knew well enough that it could cut through anything. *Not this*, the voice in her head said. *Better not . . .*

'I don't know,' she said. 'Perhaps it's not right to use the sword just to get food.'

'Just!' Edmund retorted. 'What use is the sword to us if we starve to death?'

'Right,' Cathbar agreed. 'Come on, girl; you're not going to blunt it.'

Sword? Elspeth asked in her head. There was a moment's hesitation, and then the sword flared out.

'Cut here!' called Edmund, stepping back from his place on the ice and pointing.

Elspeth reached the spot in two strides and plunged the blade down. It sliced through the surface – like cutting meat, she thought. She brought the blade around in a circle and withdrew it, leaving a round hole like an eye in the scratched grey ice. Elspeth looked down in triumph, about to call to the others, but her voice died in her throat.

There were people in the water! Dim, drifting, near-transparent figures, their great eyes reflecting the cold light of the sword. They raised slender arms towards her, calling her name. No – not her name. *Ioneth*, the faint voices chanted. *Ioneth, come to us . . .* There were so many of them . . . all the way down to the depths . . .

Hands grabbed Elspeth's shoulders and pulled her backwards. The sword flickered and died as she staggered, colliding with Fritha and Edmund, and sat down hard in the snow.

'What were you doing?' Edmund demanded. 'Another moment and you'd have fallen in!'

'Didn't you hear . . . ?' Her voice trailed off as they stared back at her. Edmund looked puzzled and concerned; Cathbar exasperated.

Only Fritha showed the beginnings of alarm. 'What?' she asked, her face tense. 'What did you hear?'

Elspeth hesitated, then risked another glance at the ice-hole. The water beneath lay black and undisturbed. 'Nothing,' she said finally. 'I was afraid the ice was cracking, that's all.'

Fritha did not look convinced, but she asked no more questions. She produced a thin rod from her pack and set-tled down by the hole to fish, watched by Edmund. Cathbar went to tend the fire. Elspeth turned away from them all and tried to calm her thoughts. She had lied to them. Well, she told herself, Cathbar would not have believed her. Edmund would think her dreaming, probably. And Fritha . . . Fritha would believe her all too well, and would be afraid. Surely the things she had seen, whatever they were, were too insub-stantial to hurt anyone! But what were they? Fritha's evil spirits?

Elspeth found herself wandering along the edge of the lake, as if movement could ease her confusion. The sun was getting low now, the little fires that dotted the shoreline glowing in the gathering shadow, but she walked on restlessly. *Fritha believes in spirits under the ice – but she didn't see them. I did; and they called to me. Why?* And what was the name they had called: Ioneth? It seemed somehow familiar, but she could not remember ever hearing it before.

'*Thu, myrk-har!*'

She jumped. The deep voice made her think of Fritha's father, Grufweld, and for a moment, disorientated, she looked around for him. But this speaker had called her *myrk-har*, black-hair, not by her name – and his voice held none of Grufweld's gentleness.

Now that she looked around, she saw that she had wandered some distance from her camp toward the tents of the fishermen. Three big, bearded men in heavy furs were standing around her. The largest was speaking again, but she could not understand him at first; something about fire. When she did not reply, he repeated himself with a scornful lilt, as if talking to an idiot. He stood a little unsteadily, she noticed, as if he had drunk too much ale.

'You're a stranger here – you should not be fishing in our lake. But Olafr here says you have a fire-stick to break the ice.'

The second man nodded and grinned, showing blackened teeth. 'It burned white, not red,' he said. 'And cut through the ice like reindeer fat!'

'So,' the first cut in, 'here's a bargain for you. Give us the fire-stick, and we won't stop you taking our fish.'

His tone was cheerful, but Elspeth had seen men like this before at the harbours. The word 'bargain' in their mouths meant: give me what you have, and I may not hurt you. Her father had been adept at sending them off without violence, but her father had been a grown man, whose position gave him respect. She could feel the sword trying to burst free,

72

sending sparks shooting up her right arm. *No!* Elspeth thought urgently. *This is the trouble we have when just one person sees you.* But the third man, wide as a hut, was blocking her way back to her own camp.

'I don't understand you!' she said, making her voice as loud as she could. Maybe Cathbar and the others would hear her – she could not see them past the wide man's shoulders. 'My . . . my father has a sword. That's how we broke the ice.'

The first man gave a bark of laughter and took a step towards her. 'That's not what Olafr saw,' he said. 'He says *you* have the stick. And as for your father's sword . . .' He half drew the long knife tucked into his belt; Olafr, beside him, sniggered and did the same. 'But we don't want a fight, do we? You're just a girl. Give us the stick now –'

A hand like a bear's paw gripped Elspeth's arm. The third man had been edging towards her as she kept her eye on the knives, and now he dragged her towards him while the other two lunged triumphantly forward. She threw herself back, trying to twist away from the fat man's grasp, and felt her feet slide out from under her. She flailed for balance, lost it and came down hard on the ice, the breath knocked out of her. A thump and a volley of curses nearby told her that the fat man had fallen with her, but the other two were bending over her, laughing. Rage filled her, and the sword flared in her hand.

She had time to see the expression in her attackers' eyes – shock, then terror – before the ground shifted under her. There was a dreadful creaking, a panicked cry from the man on the ground behind her, and then she was sliding helplessly downwards, plummeting down a shard of steeply sloping ice straight into the lake. Commotion rose all around her: screams, splashing and running footsteps. Then she was in icy water, and all sound stopped as the blackness closed over her head.

She was sinking into darkness, all light and motion fading above her. There was no air left in her: next moment she must take the ice water into her lungs . . . And then her father's voice came to her, from the days when she was small and safe, when water had been her friend: *Kick, Elspeth! Kick at it and the water will let you go the way you want. Use your arms to point the way.*

Elspeth kicked hard, casting her eyes upwards. Her arms were above her head, and over them was a greenish light . . . the sword! It still glowed, and it was pointing the way to safety. She clamped her lips shut: she *would* reach the surface . . .

Something brushed against her. She ignored it, straining upwards, but there was another touch, and then another, twining around her legs. They were all about her: the slender, translucent figures she had seen before: insubstantial but clinging; swarming up her body towards the surface . . . or else pulling her down. And a hundred soft voices sounded in her ears: *Ioneth . . . Ioneth!*

Let me go! Elspeth could not tell if it was her voice that spoke or the sword's, but her lips were still pressed together, though her lungs were on fire. Was it growing lighter above her? The whispering in her ears had become an indistinct roaring, and her body was melting with the ice.

Something wrenched painfully at her wrist. Her hair was being pulled out of her head. There was a violent yank upwards – and she was out in the blessed air, blinking in the red remains of the light, trying to breathe and coughing instead, and clinging for her life to the rough wool of Cathbar's jerkin.

'I've got you, girl,' he muttered. 'Try and stand for me now, will you? We need to get moving, fast.'

His words made no sense to her at first. She was not drowned – surely that was enough? Could she not just lie here while her body came back to her? But then she heard the other sounds, and began to see again. Edmund was standing over her, clutching his knife and looking hunted. Fritha stood nearby, an arrow fitted to her bow. Elspeth followed their gaze to see the fat man who had grabbed her lying flat on his back in the snow, wheezing and dripping wet. He must have gone through the ice as well, and his companion, the tall fisherman who had first threatened her, had only just succeeded in pulling him out. He was crouching over the fat man, very nearly as wet as he was, clutching a sodden cloak around himself and cursing at Elspeth through violently chattering teeth. And along the edge of the lake Olafr, abruptly sobered by the look of it, was leading a band of grim-faced fishermen towards them. Most of them had gutting-knives like his, and one or two had drawn them.

'Can you walk?' Cathbar asked her again. His voice was level, but there was an edge to it that Elspeth had not heard before.

An angry mutter came to her from the approaching men. She heard the word *galdra-kona*, witch, spoken in voices of anger and fear. And then Olafr's voice, shrill with fury.

'She broke the ice and pushed him in!'

'We'll see if she can drown, then,' cried another man.

'If not, she'll surely burn.'

Cathbar's voice in her ear was urgent now. 'Try to stand, Elspeth!'

But she could not stand. She could not even feel her legs. She lay helpless, the shivering starting to seize her as the men drew nearer.

CHAPTER EIGHT

Erlingr was a tall, proud fellow, near as white as his men. He scowled on me at first, saying he needed no help from the Iron people, as they call men of my race, who work with ore plundered from rocks.

But the Fay who visited me had told me true, Erlingr admitted: the chained god Loki had begun to free himself, and the land was burning and full of fear. If I could use my skill to forge new chains, he said at last, a means might be found to bind Loki again. But he would not hear of the sword, nor look at it.

The floor of the great cavern sloped downwards, and they had placed Cluaran at the lowest point, so though he was standing, his watchers looked down on him from all sides. In the many times he had been in this hall, he had never seen it so crowded: a mass of faces, pale as parchment in the dim light; most looking at him with cold hostility, though here and there a younger face that he did not recognise held simple curiosity. The light filtering through the ice wall above him bathed them in a greenish glow that made their skin and hair look translucent. *They've all come to see this*, he thought, *even the ones who weren't involved. So Erlingr has spoken to them – but what has he said? Nothing helpful, to judge by those looks.* Behind him, Ari stood impassively, more like a prison guard than an escort. It seemed there would be no help here after all. Cluaran sighed, and shifted his feet on the slippery stone.

'I've told you already, I would not have come without need,' he said again.

'And what need could be great enough to draw *you* here again?' The speaker was the oldest man there, his face so deeply lined that his cold grey eyes seemed to peer out at the world from crevices. He sat in a great carved seat in the centre of the hall, and held the yew-wood staff that by tradition was given to none but the leader of the Ice people – and Cluaran well knew the power of tradition in this place. He bowed low to the old man before replying.

'One that should concern even you, Erlingr. The dragon, *Kvöl-dreki*, is flying. It has made at least two attacks on the southern lands, and now it has carried off two children, bringing them to these mountains.'

An excited buzz rose from the listeners, and several of them rose from their ice-carved benches. Erlingr quelled them with a raised hand.

'The blue dragon has been seen by our watchers,' he

78

confirmed, ignoring the gasps from one or two of his people. 'It has flown twice over our lands, but has made no attack. Dragons have long memories, and it will remember the defeat our people inflicted on it when it last flew in war. Why should this concern us?'

'Because the two who have been kidnapped were to be taken to *Eigg Loki*, to the Chained One,' said Cluaran. The assembled Ice people fell silent. 'They are both important to him in their different ways,' he went on. 'The boy is a king's son, and his kidnap could draw an army to this land before spring comes. He is also Ripente, and I need not tell you, Erlingr, what uses the Chained One can find for their kind. But it is the girl who will be the most dangerous in his hands. She bears the crystal sword.'

There was sudden uproar. All around Cluaran, pale figures started up with exclamations of amazement, anger or disbelief. Erlingr, shouting and banging his staff, could barely quiet them. Cluaran stepped forward with both hands raised, and gradually the outcry faded to a suppressed muttering.

'I said they *were* to be taken there,' he told them. 'Watchers from among your own people saw them escape the dragon. Ari, here, can confirm that.' Ari, behind him, made a sound of assent as Cluaran continued. 'They are alive, wandering somewhere on the ice plain – but they are being hunted as we speak. That is why I have come here: to find them and help them, before they are captured. This girl has the means to destroy our common enemy once and for all. But the sword is also the only thing that could break his chains. If he can capture her and bind her, he will escape.'

The crowd were silent now. Cluaran raised his head, appealing to them with all the skill he could muster. 'Remember that it was your people as much as mine who bound him before – and if he is freed, he will want his revenge.' He sent his voice ringing through the cavern. 'Will you help me?'

Now the faces turned to Erlingr. There was a low muttering: *Do we help him? Do we believe him?*

'Ari,' the old man commanded. 'Come forward.' The green-eyed man cast an unreadable glance at Cluaran as he moved to stand beside him.

'You have seen these children,' Erlingr said. 'Is it true? Does this . . . human girl bear the crystal sword?'

There was a long pause. 'I have not seen it,' Ari said at last. 'But I believe that she does. A bright light was seen in the girl's hand as the dragon carried her. Even to have escaped him, to have survived for this long, they must have some help, some weapon of a more than common nature. And Cluaran has seen –'

'I did not ask what *he* says he has seen,' the old man broke in. 'Nor what you believe.' Erlingr rose to his feet, a full head taller than Cluaran, and turned to address his people. 'Is it likely, do you think, that the sword would give itself to a child . . . to one of the short-lived ones, in a country so far from its forging? And what could such a one do with it? Are we to believe that a human girl could kill the Chained One – or that she could release him? No. I would rather ask –' he brought the staff down with a crack on the ice – 'why, now the dragon is flying again, we see *this man's* return to the land he has wronged?'

The old man threw Cluaran a look of undisguised contempt. 'Tell us no more stories, man without a people; soft-talker; betrayer! Have you come here to kill more of our kind?'

Cluaran had been ready for this. He kept the anger out of his voice as he answered: 'I killed none of yours, Erlingr. You know well who it was who murdered your men. But for their sacrifice, no one here would be alive today.'

Erlingr's face twisted. 'Their sacrifice, yes – and ours; and mine! A whole line was wiped out by your fine words!'

'It was *Loki* who killed your son and grandsons!' Cluaran snapped at him. 'And he would have destroyed much more –'

'*We do not speak that name here!*' the old man thundered. He strode across the floor to Cluaran and glared down at him, the staff raised as if about to strike him. Abruptly he seemed to recollect himself and lowered the staff.

'Ingvald and my grandsons died in battle, that is true,' he said quietly, but with undiminished bitterness. 'While *you* came back without hurt. And there was one more, one last remnant of my line, taken from me by you – by your companion and his . . . *workmanship*.' He spat out the last word as if it scalded him.

'Your granddaughter was *not* of your line!' Cluaran could

not hide his anger now. 'She was not even of the true race, you said. You had no value for her! You called her earth-born . . .' He stopped, not trusting himself to say more, but still holding Erlingr's eyes. He felt a dismal kind of triumph when the old man looked down first.

'I did blame Ingvald when he adopted the child,' Erlingr muttered. 'But after his death, she was the last thing remaining to me.' He met Cluaran's gaze again, and the minstrel was startled to see a glitter like tears in the old man's eyes. 'You should not have taken her.'

'I did not,' Cluaran said very quietly. 'It was her choice, and not my will.' He could see in those glittering eyes that Erlingr would never believe him. Behind the old man the Ice people were straining to hear what was being said, but Cluaran knew there would be no reaching them now. All that he could do was leave quickly – if he was allowed.

He realised that someone else was speaking, and for a moment was shocked to hear a voice other than Erlingr's and his own. It was Ari, his voice slow and rough as if he were dragging it over stones. 'It was her choice. And some of us honour and love her for it still. For her sake, Erlingr, I will go with Cluaran, if you allow it.'

Erlingr looked down at the two of them in lowering silence. Then abruptly, he turned his back on them and stumped back to his seat, to face his pale followers. He raised his staff in a signal that brought them all to their feet, watching him in silence.

'The man may go!' he proclaimed, his voice filling the hall. 'For the sake of the friendship that was once between us, I will not be the one to kill him. But for the sake of his past betrayal, he goes unhelped and unprovided. Let him leave now, and do not speak to him.'

The old man turned one last time to Cluaran. 'Go,' he said heavily. 'No one will hinder you. Go to *Eigg Loki*, and die there – alone, unless this fool truly means to follow you. But I will not send one more man to die with you.'

He sank into his chair, lowering his head and closing his eyes. His people remained standing, though when Cluaran swept his gaze over the massed rows, none would look at him. He turned from them and walked away, his footsteps echoing loudly in the silence. After a moment he heard Ari follow. All the way down the tunnel that led to the outside air, the silence pursued them, and the weight of five hundred eyes at their backs.

CHAPTER NINE

The black-haired girl, Ioneth, brought us food. She told us she was not of Erlingr's people: her own race, the people of rock and ice, had been destroyed twelve years before, when Loki first sent out his fires. All were burned . . . all but Ioneth. Erlingr's son Ingvald found the child wandering among the ashes, and took her in as his own.

Later, Ioneth took me out to the snow fields and showed me mountains on the horizon, white-peaked, but streaked with black.

– There is *Eigg Loki*, she said, where the demon is chained, though perhaps not for long. And then she whispered, so low that I wondered if I had heard her right:

– I can help you kill him.

'Please try to walk, Elspeth!'

Edmund and Cathbar between them had hauled Elspeth upright, but her knees kept buckling under her, and she looked at Edmund without recognition. *If only we'd got here sooner!* he thought desperately. The sound that the ice made as it cracked kept ringing in his mind. He had plunged head and arms into the water, trying to catch Elspeth as she slid out of sight, but it was not until Cathbar arrived that they had been able to reach her.

Had they been too late after all? Elspeth had not spoken since they had pulled her from the water; her eyes seeming to focus only on her right hand, where a pale glow was all that remained of the sword. Her lips were bluish and she shivered uncontrollably, despite the blankets they had draped around her.

The fishermen were close enough now for Edmund to distinguish individual voices. He did not understand the words, but he could hear the threat in their tone – and see it in their drawn knives as they trudged nearer along the shoreline, not running but keeping close together, as if stalking a dangerous animal. Their leader, a stocky man with a red beard and blackened teeth, yelled something at them, his voice harsh with rage.

'They don't even know us! Why are they doing this?' Edmund muttered to Cathbar. But he knew the answer even before the captain's eyes flicked towards Elspeth's hand. They had both seen the struggle on the ice after Elspeth cried out, and seen the flash of the sword as they started towards her.

They had left the ice and were back on the trodden snow that covered firm ground. Fritha, a few feet ahead of them, was leading them back along the lake's edge towards their campsite. Then something whirred past Edmund's head and he heard Fritha cry out in fear. The men were throwing stones at them. Desperation sharpened his voice as he turned back to Elspeth. 'You must walk! They want to take the sword from you!'

Her eyes widened in alarm, and he saw the life come back to her face. Beside him, Cathbar grunted in relief as Elspeth, grimacing, put one foot down, then the other.

Fritha called out again to Cathbar, glancing over her shoulder at the approaching men. The tall girl's face was white and set, but her voice was steady. Cathbar replied with a nod, and turned to Edmund.

'She says to follow where she goes!'

Fritha broke into a run. The nearest pursuers were only yards from Edmund and Cathbar now, and the two of them broke into a shuffling trot after her, lifting Elspeth off her feet once again as they tried to keep up. But the tall girl did not lead them back to their fire. Instead, she turned back on to the ice, walking straight out towards the centre of the lake.

'Not that way!' Edmund shouted in horror. 'What if the ice cracks again?'

'That's what they'll be thinking, too,' Cathbar told him, jerking his head at the pursuing men, who had slowed their chase and were shouting and pointing.

Fritha was testing each step, heading further and further away from the shore, towards the shadowy mass of the mountain. In a few moments Cathbar, Edmund and Elspeth had reached the spot at which she had ventured on to the ice. Without hesitation, Cathbar headed after her, dragging the other two with him.

'It's safer than meeting *them*,' the captain said shortly, darting a glance over his shoulder. 'They're calling us thieves – and they want to drown Elspeth for a witch.'

A howl rose from the fishermen as they saw what their quarry was doing. Fritha moved steadily forward without turning her head, sliding one foot at a time through the light covering of snow and leaving two dark trails behind her. The other three followed in her tracks, clutching each other for balance as their feet slid on the smooth surface. Edmund tried not to hear the shouts and jeers of the men behind them, or to think about the ice cracking beneath his feet. He kept his eyes on Fritha's back and fixed all his attention on staying upright, keeping hold of Elspeth and moving ahead, step by slippery step.

The men did not follow them on to the ice. The shouting behind them stopped for a moment, then began again with a new intensity. Something stung Edmund's arm, and something else hissed as it hit the ground at his feet. He turned his head and saw the men clustered at the edge of the ice, shouting and catcalling like spectators at a wrestling match. Several had their hands raised. They were throwing . . . it couldn't be stones; where could they find stones, here? They had opened up one of their iron melting-pans with thickly gloved hands, and were throwing lumps of glowing charcoal on to the ice.

The red-bearded leader shouted in triumph as a lump grazed Edmund's shoulder, singeing his fur sleeve and almost hitting Elspeth. Fritha turned her head, and called out a frantic instruction.

'Stay close!' Cathbar bellowed. 'They're trying to crack the ice – it's much thinner here than near the bank! Fritha says she can find us a safe path, but we've got to keep together!'

Edmund lunged forward, and Elspeth, still supported between the two of them, found the strength to keep pace. Fritha had abandoned her cautious progress and was gliding over the ice ahead, almost out of reach of the missiles already. But hot charcoal was falling all around Edmund, and he could go no faster. Elspeth's weight dragged at him and his feet skidded at every step in the loose snow. Two burning lumps landed in front of him, sizzling and making round holes in the ice. He staggered as Cathbar swerved to avoid the holes and almost fell, dragging Elspeth with him. Smoke rose to catch in his throat and an ominous creaking sounded beneath his feet.

'Don't run, Edmund,' Cathbar shouted. '*Slide* your feet, like her.' He jerked his chin to indicate Fritha – then cursed as a glowing coal caught in the fur of his cloak, and he had to beat it out, one-handed.

Edmund straightened up as well as he could and tried to imitate Fritha's graceful motion. Elspeth, still leaning on his shoulder, seemed to be concentrating on her own feet as she tried not to fall. The shouts and jeers behind them seemed louder than ever, but he would not look back. Surely they must be nearly out of range by now?

From the shore, the sound of their tormentors stopped abruptly. Next moment, the surface under Edmund's feet began to tilt. Three burning coals, landing close together, had done their work. A crack was opening up beside him, black water welling over the grey ice, and he felt himself sliding helplessly towards it.

'*Fall flat!*' Cathbar bellowed. Before Edmund could react the captain had knocked his feet from under him, giving him a shove so that he flew forward and landed on his face. Elspeth landed near him, and then, with a thud, Cathbar himself. 'Crawl!' the man yelled at them. 'Get away from the hole!'

A roaring filled Edmund's ears as he hauled himself along the ice, scrabbling for a purchase with knees and elbows as his fingers went numb. The fishermen on the shore were howling, baying like wolves at the kill. But the surface beneath Edmund held firm. Then Fritha's hand closed over his, and he was yanked away from the crack, back on to level ice. A few feet away, Cathbar was supporting Elspeth as she clambered to her knees. The shrill yells of triumph behind them changed to growls of disappointment, and Edmund knew they had won.

As Fritha helped him to his feet, he risked a glance back at the shore. The men stood in a ragged huddle, arguing. As he watched, several of them turned away, starting to walk back along the shoreline to the fires of their camp. There were angry yells from the group that remained, and one of the leavers turned to shout back at them. Edmund made out the words '*Eigg Loki*'. He looked at Fritha, who had been listening beside him.

'Some of them leave now,' she said. But her face was pale. 'They say that we will die anyway, because we go toward *Eigg Loki*. The spirits in the mountain will kill us.'

Edmund knew Fritha was very afraid, more than she would ever admit. He remembered her tales of spirits who lured the unwary to their deaths in the mountain and in the lakes and crevasses around it – and it was this very lake that had killed her mother. How could she go any further with them?

'*You* don't have to . . .' he began awkwardly. 'I mean, you've done all you said you would, and more. Shouldn't you go back to your father?'

'Edmund's right.' It was Elspeth, standing with her hand on Cathbar's arm and speaking for the first time since her rescue. Her voice was weak but steady. 'I'm more grateful than I can say. You've put yourself to such trouble and danger to bring us here. But you must not come any further.' She moved away from Cathbar, swaying a little. 'In fact, I think none of you should. It'll be dangerous inside the mountain. The sword will keep me safe, but you . . .'

'I'm not going back now!' Edmund exclaimed indignantly. 'How could you think it?'

Fritha was silent, looking up at the dark mass of the mountain ahead of them. Edmund had been too concerned with their escape to notice how close they had come to it, but now it blotted out the sky: bare rock scored with crevasses, almost black in the evening light. To one side of the mountain a glacier fell, a tumbled, pitted sheet of lighter grey, reflecting red glints in the last of the sun. Fritha stared at the scene for some moments, then shook her head. She spoke to Elspeth in her own language, then translated to Edmund.

'I will stay too. How can I tell my father I leave you at *Eigg Loki*?' She gave him a brief smile. 'And I want to know what will happen.'

'So that's all of us,' Cathbar put in. 'I'm here to protect you both, and if there's danger, so much the more need. And to tell the truth, girl, you're not too steady on your legs yet.' He took Elspeth's arm again, and although she shook her head at first, she was clearly grateful for the support. 'So if we're heading for this mountain, shall we be moving? I'd be glad to get off the ice before it's quite dark.'

They made better progress now the fear of pursuit had gone. As night fell a sharp breeze began to blow, which swept the ice surface clear of much of its covering of snow. Edmund soon mastered the technique of sliding, and Cathbar, though he seemed clumsy, managed to stay upright. Only Elspeth still fell, though she always scrambled up without help and would not let them wait for her, seeming angry and impatient at her weakness. A half-moon had risen behind them, and in the blackness above the stars looked down like fierce little eyes. They gave small light, but the ice beneath the travellers' feet gleamed with its own pale radiance. So did the side of *Eigg Loki* ahead of them, where the great glacier swept down to meet the frozen lake. The ice river grew steadily closer, and suddenly there were jumbled boulders at their feet, with a great tilted plain of ice to one side, sloping upwards higher than Edmund could follow with his eyes.

'*Eigg Loki*,' Fritha said softly. 'But we must take care. The *nithingar* are here.'

She was looking off to one side, along the foot of the mountain. Following her gaze, Edmund saw a dark area against the grey rock that might be a cave, and deep within it, an orange point of light. Fritha's face was tense, and she gestured for them to speak low. She said something rapidly to Cathbar, who translated for the other two.

'It's a community of men who have been thrown out of their villages for serious crimes: killing, mostly. They band together in the woods and caves, and live by trapping and hunting, and thieving.' His face wrinkled in disgust. 'She says they've an evil reputation, and I can well believe it. Men without family, or master, or clan!'

'They rob travellers sometimes,' Fritha said. 'We should not meet them.'

Elspeth was already picking her way through the boulders at the mountain's foot. 'It's just someone's campfire,' she said. 'Why should they be robbers?'

'No one else would camp on *Eigg Loki*,' Fritha said simply. 'No one but *rekingar*, men with no place.'

And us, thought Edmund.

Cathbar had joined Elspeth, scouting for a way up the mountain, while Fritha walked a little way on to the ice lake, using one of her blankets to sweep over as many of their footprints as she could reach. She kept looking at the faint glow of the fire. 'We should keep quiet now,' she said softly. 'They are bad men.'

'But we have nothing to steal!' Edmund said.

Fritha only shook her head. She stopped brushing out their footprints and led him through the rocks to Elspeth and Cathbar. 'I will show you how to climb up,' she said. 'You want to go inside the mountain?' Elspeth nodded. Fritha swallowed hard before speaking again; then she pointed out a place between two jagged boulders, at the edge of the glacier.

'We can start climbing there,' she said. 'My mother showed me once, before . . . Higher up, there is a way into the mountain, under the ice.' She handed Cathbar the dirty, ice-stiffened blanket. 'Take this,' she told him. 'You go last, and wipe out the footprints.' Then she began picking her way over the rocky ground, keeping to the edge of the ice as she led them upwards.

The wind had swept the rocks clear of snow, and although Edmund's legs ached and the cold was creeping through his boots and gloves, the climb felt easy at first. The mountain rose from the ice fields in a series of rough boulders, offering good footing, and above them there was a track of sorts, a shallow depression running through the grey stones. Cathbar had no need to erase their footprints now; he had slung the blanket over his shoulder as he walked, slowly but steadily, just behind Edmund. Ahead of him, Elspeth seemed to have recovered completely from her near-drowning, and strode forward as if in a hurry. Beyond her, Edmund could dimly see Fritha's back. The tall girl was holding herself very straight, and Edmund wondered what she was thinking.

Suddenly Fritha stopped and turned. 'The *nithingar* – they have seen us and are following!' she hissed.

Elspeth gave a small exclamation of annoyance as she nearly collided with her, but she looked at Fritha's face and fell silent. They stood stock-still, listening intently – and then Edmund heard it too.

Voices – several of them, speaking in harsh whispers.

The sound came from below them: Edmund could not tell how far below. Cathbar, standing like a statue just behind him, leant forward to put his mouth to Edmund's ear.

'Look in on them,' he murmured. 'Tell me how many – and what weapons.'

Edmund nodded, and sent his sight out to where the voices were.

He was no more than twenty paces below the track, in a natural shelter between huge boulders. He could see three men – no, four, leaning as if at ease against the great stones, waiting for their leader's word to advance on their prey just above. All had long knives in their belts. The man whose eyes he had borrowed looked down at the scabbard at his own side, and Edmund felt the man's cruel satisfaction as his eyes rested on the fine bronze hilt, and a flash of the pleasure he had felt when he killed its previous owner.

'Five,' Edmund muttered. 'Knives, and one sword.'

Cathbar nodded, but Edmund stayed looking at their attackers a moment longer. He flicked to another man's eyes – hunger, impatience and a longing to attack now – and back to the leader. There was no impatience in his mind, only readiness, and expectation. Expecting what? Edmund wondered – and then he had it. The man was not thinking of battle – he meant to ambush the travellers while they slept.

Edmund regained his own eyes and stared along the track ahead of them. It carried on for maybe another fifty paces, a wavering line just visible between two banks of rocks, but then the rock walls rose and closed in on each side, rising steeply again. A sliver of moon, high above, glinted off sheer planes and jagged edges: it looked a foolhardy climb to attempt at night. But just before the rise, the track seemed to widen . . .

Edmund reached out to grasp Elspeth by the arm, pointing urgently while he tried to speak with no breath. 'They think we'll camp just there! That's when they plan to attack. But if we don't stop . . .'

Elspeth nodded briefly and whispered a few words to Fritha. The tall girl set off at once, moving rapidly but in complete silence. Edmund hoped she would be able to guide them as swiftly up the lethal-looking slope in front of them. If they could just reach it before the *nithingar* realised that their intended victims had not stopped . . . maybe the men would not attempt the climb in darkness, or maybe Fritha could find them a safe ledge from which they could fight . . . though there was no sign of any ledge on the black cliff that loomed ahead.

Edmund crept onwards, trying not to think of falling from the rock, or of the knives of the men just below them. *Make no sound*, he told himself, bringing each foot down as softly as he could . . . but he could not quieten the sound of his own heart thundering in his ears.

The hunt was on again.

CHAPTER TEN

A year before this, Ioneth said, three strangers came to visit Erlingr.

They told him of a sword that was being forged in the southern lands, which would have the power to kill Loki. The blade would unite the endurance of stone, the sharpness of metal, and wood's power to heal itself. And when the sword came here, it must take into its substance something of the Ice people. They asked Erlingr to find one who was willing to give his life to the sword.

Erlingr sent them away, but the thought stayed with her that she – Ioneth – might be the one they sought. And she crept after the strangers, and asked them what she must do.

Edmund had wished it was still daylight when they began scrambling up the mountain, but now he was glad of the darkness. He had felt horribly visible as they crept up the remaining track, and still more so when the rocks closed in and they were forced to scramble. It was almost as hard as he had feared. The weak moonlight showed the outline of each rock, but not the smaller obstacles. Edmund felt desperately for footholds, banging his shins and elbows against unseen snags, and fearing that every slight sound would alert the *nithingar* below. When Elspeth, just ahead of him, trod awkwardly and sent a shower of loose pebbles towards him, he lost his footing, sprawled for a moment on the rough stone, and involuntarily looked down. He was sure he caught a movement on the path below – but there was still no sound, and he forced himself to focus only on the climb.

'It gets narrow here – be careful!' Fritha called softly from above.

Edmund signalled frantically at her, telling her to be quiet, but she had already turned back to the rock face. A few paces further on, Edmund saw what she meant. A gap had opened up between the mountain and the ice to their left; the rock fell away in a narrow fissure, while the ice stuck out above it in a shelf more than a foot wide. To the right, another stream of ice now flowed, its surface steep and glassy-smooth. Above him, Elspeth had slowed her pace as she searched for handholds and footholds. And suddenly, shockingly, there were voices below them – no longer stealthy whispers but harsh cries of anger and surprise, and running feet. The *nithingar* had realised that their prey were escaping.

Elspeth's eyes widened. She hauled herself up with reckless speed to join Fritha. Edmund scrambled to use the same handholds that she had used, suddenly conscious of his own heavy breathing and that of Cathbar behind him.

Fritha spoke quietly to Elspeth, who passed the message down. 'She says that just above is where the track turns under the ice, into the mountain. But it's a steep drop and very dangerous in the dark: we should really wait for daylight. She doesn't think they'll dare to come up this far.'

'We'll wait,' said Cathbar.

It did seem as if the men below them were unnerved. As the voices came nearer, Edmund could hear them arguing. He stood pressed against the rock, listening, his head a bare inch from Elspeth's foot. He heard the word *uvettar* – 'evil spirits' – several times, spoken in tones of fear and anger. At length there was a clatter of movement from below, and at the same moment he felt a tug on his sleeve as Cathbar pulled himself up.

'Go higher!' the captain hissed. 'They're saying there are spirits in the rock here, and we must have something worth stealing to take such a risk. Find a place above to hide – *go!*'

Edmund's heart was thumping afresh as he relayed the message to Elspeth. She only nodded as if she had expected this, but he wondered how Fritha must be feeling as she began the ascent again. He tried to peer up beyond Elspeth's legs, but everything above her was lost in the darkness.

At least the climb was a little easier here. Fritha led them up a series of ledges almost like steps, broader though steeper than the track below. To their left, the crevice still yawned, growing deeper and wider so that the shelf of ice above no longer covered it and its bottom was lost in darkness. Edmund found himself huddling against the ice stream to his right as he climbed, and saw Elspeth above him doing the same. Fear had banished his earlier tiredness; there was nothing now but the climb, the black rock and moonlit ice . . . and the crunch of pursuing boots below them.

Then, without warning, Fritha stopped. Edmund saw Elspeth hesitate, then haul herself up so that she stood beside their guide, and found that he could do the same. They had reached the broadest ledge yet, so wide that it might have been cut deliberately in the stone as a resting place – but above it the rock wall rose sheer, higher than Fritha's head, with no visible handhold. Following Fritha's gaze, Edmund saw that this was where the crevice ended. To their right the ledge on which they stood was cut off by the stream of ice, but to their left both rock wall and ledge ran onwards, facing the chasm and disappearing into the darkness under the ice shelf. There was no other way to go.

Fritha muttered something in her own language, staring out along the ledge. Her face was blank with terror and she stood as if paralysed. It wrenched Edmund to see her so helpless, and without thinking he pushed past Elspeth to go to her. As he did, Cathbar hauled himself half-up beside them. The captain looked up at the impassable rock wall and shook his head.

'They're still coming,' he said softly. 'They're frightened, and that makes them more angry. But they can't see us from where they are. You go down that ledge – just out of sight where the moonlight stops – and hold still. I'll try to get away without fighting – scare 'em off with a ghost tale.' But Edmund noticed that he checked his sword hilt as he spoke. 'If not,' Cathbar added, 'you'll have to get to Fritha's cave without me. Make your stand there, if it comes to it. Feel your way with your feet, and *go slow* – they won't run, not up here.' He gave them a last urgent look, and lowered himself back down the rock face.

Fritha was still motionless, staring wide-eyed into the darkness. Edmund slipped past her and took her hand.

'Come on,' he said. 'I'll go first.' And without giving himself time to think, he edged out along the ledge towards the chasm, pulling her with him. He heard Elspeth's small exclamation of surprise as she followed.

The stone was rough underfoot, but firm. Fritha walked next to him as if she had no will of her own, her face fixed and staring at nothing. Remembering how she had led them over the ice fields, Edmund moved with exaggerated caution, testing each step before he trusted his weight to it, scanning the rock wall for obstacles or handholds . . . not letting himself think of what followed behind them, or what waited ahead; not looking down. Below them was thick darkness, more terrible than any jagged rocks. '*Úminni-gjar*,' Fritha had called the crevices: forgetting-places. A single step into that blackness and you would vanish as if you had never been. *Stop that*, he chided himself. *They depend on you now!* One more step, then another.

The next step took him into complete darkness. They had reached the ice shelf: a massive roof of grey ice met the rock wall behind them and cut off the moonlight. Fritha stopped abruptly, her hand tightening in his.

'The spirits are in there,' she murmured.

'Just two more steps,' he whispered, trying to sound reassuring. 'Just out of the light – then we'll stop. We can go back after Cathbar sends the men away.'

She bit back a whimper of panic, but followed him into the dark. Elspeth, stepping quickly behind her, put a hand on her shoulder. Edmund could see no fear in Elspeth's face, only a strange eagerness, almost a hunger. They stood huddled together, pressing their backs against the cold stone, looking back at the moonlit mountainside and listening.

For what seemed an age, there was no sound at all. Then Edmund heard faint voices: Cathbar, speaking in a tone of great reasonableness; another man sounding alarmed and angry. Cathbar's voice became more vehement; there was a small chorus of exclamations; and then one voice – the leader, he thought – cut through the rest in a shout: '*Skrok-mathr!*' He was calling Cathbar a liar. Next moment, they heard the metallic clash of blades.

Edmund turned to Fritha and found her looking at him, her face ghostly in the darkness. 'We should help him!' she whispered.

'We have to go on,' Elspeth said firmly. 'That's what he said.'

She couldn't mean it, Edmund thought. Surely the crystal sword could defeat five men. 'But they'll kill Cathbar if we don't help!'

Elspeth stood like a stone. Edmund glared at her, about to insist – and saw an icy distance in her eyes that choked the words in his throat.

'We must go further in,' she said.

Edmund felt his way along the ledge, full of resentment and worry. Fritha followed him, shivering. It was as black as a tunnel now: the roof of ice cut out all light and he could not see the chasm that must still gape just beyond his feet. He stopped, holding Fritha's arm and peering into the blackness until he could make out the surface of the rock again, and the wavering grey line of the ledge stretching ahead of him. And something else: somewhere in the distance the grey line gave way to a black spike surrounded by less intense darkness, like an opening in rock or ice.

The clashes and cries behind them grew louder. Edmund risked a look back to where the moon still shone at the tunnel's entrance. Elspeth had not moved: she was standing very still, close to the opening, looking intently down at her right hand. Beyond her, Cathbar was clambering up to the ledge, a small black figure silvered by moonlight. Another figure climbed after him, the moon glittering on a long blade in its hand, but Cathbar gained his feet and kicked out, sending his pursuer sprawling back. There were grunts and curses below him, and then two men were scrambling up, the first lunging with his knife while the second tried to hook Cathbar's legs from under him. The captain sidestepped, brought his sword round – a shrill yell told them he had hit home – and caught the knife-wielder on his weapon arm with a shove that almost sent the man over the edge into the crevice. The attacker dropped out of sight, flailing, and Cathbar turned to call blindly along the ledge.

'Make for the cave! I'm coming after you!'

There was a dazzling flash of light. Edmund staggered for an instant and forced himself back against the rock wall, throwing out an arm to steady Fritha. Elspeth was still standing near the opening, brilliantly lit by the crystal sword, which had sprung to life in her hand. As Edmund and Fritha watched, she moved as if sleepwalking back to where the ice roof began, and raised the sword over her head.

'NO!' Edmund screamed. He had seen the sword cut through rock before now. It would be a small matter for it to cause an ice-fall from the overhang, to block the ledge and leave Cathbar to the bandits and their knives. 'ELSPETH! What are you doing?'

Elspeth started violently, looking at her arm as if it did not belong to her. Then slowly, with effort and fury visible on her face, she lowered her arm and stood for a moment, breathing hard. She made her way back towards Edmund and Fritha, the sword held stiffly down at her side, while Cathbar, his face bewildered, came after her.

'You would have killed Cathbar!' Edmund hissed at Elspeth as she reached them. 'What were you thinking?'

'I don't know,' she murmured. 'The sword . . . it seemed to be . . .'

'Don't stand there mithering!' Cathbar yelled, lumbering along the ledge towards them. '*Run!*'

Their pursuers had not missed the appearance of the sword. There were yells of amazement, and three of them clambered up to the ledge, pointing and shouting. The other two, both apparently wounded, joined them more slowly. The leader began to move along the ledge, shouting abuse at Cathbar, closely followed by his uninjured companions. Edmund grabbed Fritha's hand and began to pull her towards the ice wall at the end of the ledge, the narrow entrance in it now clearly visible in the sword's light.

And then suddenly there was a noise like ripping cloth – a sound Edmund had heard before, knew at once – and the men behind them started to scream as the moon and stars beyond the ice roof were blotted out. Through the opening an eye looked in at Edmund, bigger than the moon, the black streak across it seeming to focus its cold hatred directly on him. His legs turned to water.

Torment.

'Run!' Fritha shouted, pushing him forward.

The dragon's roar shook the stone under Edmund's feet.

He staggered, nearly fell but regained his balance and reached the cave entrance in a dozen steps. He collapsed with Fritha on the icy floor as Elspeth and Cathbar raced along the ledge towards them. Behind them the dragon picked one of the *nithingar* off the ledge and held him struggling in its claw as it shot a jet of blue flame directly at the ice roof. Next moment everything was lost to view in a storm of falling rock and ice.

For an instant the dragon felt the old joy of the hunt as it swooped on its prey. There were some of them down on the rocks, exposed and there for the taking. And under the glacier were the ones it had been sent to find, the ones who had hurt it . . .

No, the voice in its head commanded, *you must leave those. The others you can have.*

The dragon let out a roar that shook one of the little figures off the ledge, to fall away, down, down into the chasm. But it managed to grasp another in its talons, and saw one more running back to the rocks, where it could be caught later. The dragon beat its wings lightly, hovering in the air above its squealing prey. There was one final command, and it sent a burst of flame into the edge of the glacier, bringing down rock and ice to trap the little creatures beneath . . . Then, freed for a while from the voice, it flew down, finally, to feast.

CHAPTER ELEVEN

– I am all my people, Ioneth said: a whole race of ice dwellers. What better spirit could you find to guide your sword?

I turned from her, telling myself I would forget the sword I had laboured over for so long, and forge chains instead, to bind the demon for a while longer.

I could not sacrifice her. Young though she was, she had a light in her that all could see: she shone out among those pale folk like an eagle among geese. I could tell my boy liked her, too, though he tried to hide it from me – and I thought she liked him.

For a while, all four of them lay where they had thrown themselves on the floor of the cave. The sword still glowed brightly, showing them the two walls of their refuge: one of rock, one of ice; both grey, meeting somewhere far above their heads. Nothing showed beyond the cave's entrance; not a single gleam of moon or stars. Perhaps the dragon's attack had sealed it off – but for the moment Elspeth was too tired to get up and look. This was where she was meant to be, the sole aim of their past days of travel – and suddenly her mind was filled with doubts. It was the sword that had told her to come here: the sword that had gradually become a part of her. She could not remember now exactly when it had happened: the blade feeling like part of her own arm; the sword's voice in her head becoming as familiar to her as her own thoughts.

But they were *not* her own, she told herself fiercely. She could still hear the voice in her head: *They must not follow! Hurry – block the path!* She had seen in her head the picture of what she must do, and without thinking, without question, she had gone to do it . . . If Edmund had not called out, she would have killed Cathbar, her protector, many times over – sacrificed him to a purpose she didn't fully understand.

You do understand it, the sword told her. *We are here to kill Loki. You've known that ever since the dragon took you – but you would not say the words before.*

The others were climbing to their feet, groaning and exclaiming at their escape.

'Where now?' Edmund asked.

He was looking at Elspeth. She started – but of course, they had no guide now. Fritha had never been here – should not be here at all, she thought, looking at the girl's terrified face. She knew the paths up the mountain, but neither she nor any of her people would willingly venture into its heart. No: it was Elspeth who had led them inside *Eigg Loki*, and they expected her to know where to go. The sword's voice rang in her head again, but she shut it out for the moment.

'I think we should explore,' she said to Edmund. A distant roaring sounded somewhere outside: the dragon, still hunting. 'Find a safe place where we can rest,' she added. 'We can use the sword for light.' *But not for directions*, she told herself; *not until I know it won't threaten anyone else*.

Cathbar, leaning against the rock wall, looked at the sword with a new wariness, and did not speak to Elspeth as she led the way deeper into the narrow cave. He was wounded again, she saw: a deep cut on his burned face, and a bloody gash on his arm. His silence was hard to bear – but what could she say to him?

The ground was rock, not ice, and the walls narrowed to a tunnel as they walked on, cutting deep into the mountain. Darkness pooled around them, the sword's light showing only an endless stretch of rough stone to each side. It was absolutely quiet now, their footsteps the only sound. Edmund talked a little to Fritha, asking how she was, but the ice seemed to muffle their voices, and soon they walked in silence.

I did know the sword's purpose, Elspeth thought. *It was created to defeat Loki; Cluaran told us that. How could that mean anything other than killing him? And if that's what I must do, I think I could do it. But not if it means killing my friends!*

She glanced at the little group behind her. Cathbar was walking at the back, holding his arm stiffly.

He's one man. The sword's voice whipped through her head before she could block it. *Loki has killed thousands, and if he is freed he means to burn the world. How can you set one life against that?*

Elspeth stopped, so suddenly that Edmund collided with her. 'How can I . . . ?' she echoed out loud.

Edmund and Fritha looked at her, startled, and she deliberately lowered the sword.

Like this, she said in her head, and she clenched her hand as if to crush it. *Go! Leave me! You will not throw away my friends' lives for your plan!*

The sword vanished – and they were plunged into darkness. Behind her, Edmund exclaimed and Fritha gave a small cry of terror. There was a moment of silence – then slowly, reluctantly, Elspeth opened her hand to let the clear light spill out again. *I can't let them walk in the dark*, she told the sword. *But try to control me again, and I will shut you out.*

'What happened just then?' said Edmund, his voice not quite steady.

'I'm sorry.' Elspeth kept her voice calm. 'I lost my concentration for a moment. I'm fine now.'

There was something else, though, as they moved slowly on through the stone tunnel. In the darkness, she was sure she had seen drifting white shapes ahead of them, clinging to the walls. Now, in the light cast by the sword, the shapes were gone.

The ground began to slope upward and their steps became

slower. Fritha stumbled, and Elspeth realised she was staggering with weariness.

'Let's stop for a while,' she called, and all four sank
gratefully down against the rock wall.

Fritha had a tense, wary look that Elspeth had not seen on
her before, like a cat before a storm. Edmund seemed intent
on cheering her, asking her questions about charcoal-burning
and the way to cure a wolfskin – but not, Elspeth realised,
anything about the tales of ghosts and spirits that had so
interested him before they came to the mountain. Elspeth was
not so sure, now, that those stories were fables. Her father had
always scoffed at the sailors' tales of sirens that enticed a man
and then dragged him down – but what of the creatures she
herself had met, under the ice? Her clothes had long since
dried, but she shivered at the memory. The drifting shapes she
had glimpsed in that moment of darkness had looked like the
creatures in the lake, and had twined around each other in the
same way.

Cathbar spoke, the first words Elspeth had heard from him
since they entered the cave. 'Don't know if any of you have
noticed it, but there's light somewhere up ahead. Maybe we
can give that sword a rest.'

Elspeth could not read his expression, but she felt warm
with relief to hear his voice again. 'I hope so!' she said
fervently, and hoped he might understand.

Now that Cathbar had drawn attention to the light, they
all saw it: a faint, greenish tinge to the darkness that showed

up as the smallest gleam on tiny irregularities on the walls to each side. The thought of some natural light cheered all of them, and they clambered to their feet again. The path became much steeper and more rocky, and soon they were scrambling up a series of natural steps, while all the time the greenish light grew brighter. And then they were at the top, in a passage seemingly roofed with ice, for the light appeared to come down through it.

'We're under the glacier,' Fritha whispered.

Elspeth gratefully let the sword fade – and then hesitated. Ahead of her, just as before, was a white, insubstantial form, drifting like smoke . . . but she would have said it looked human if it had stayed still long enough. None of the others seemed to have noticed it. They pressed eagerly forward, walking abreast of her as the passage widened to a cavern.

Fritha screamed.

The cavern was walled with the writhing forms – there was no mistaking them now. They hung in the air like ice dust, each one human in form, long and thin, with great hollow eye-spaces glowing green in the chamber's light. They gathered around the travellers like moths drawn to a flame.

'*Tæl-draugar!*' Fritha gasped. The creatures from her stories: grave-dwellers who sucked the life from unwary visitors. She flailed at them, but her arms went through them. All four of them had backed into the corridor, but the smoky creatures came with them, clustering about them so thickly that they were losing sight of each other. One was trying to push inside

Elspeth's mouth, feeling like icy smoke. In panic she called for the sword and it flared in her hand, but its light was dim and faint, overshadowed by the glow that came from the spirits themselves. The things were drawn by it, though – just as the water creatures had been. They drew away from her face and body to cluster around the blade, though none of them came close enough to touch it.

In seconds Elspeth was the centre of a whirlpool of the creatures, and a thousand voiceless whispers breathed a name she had heard before: *Ioneth*. There was no more substance to them than smoke, but there were so many of them . . . flocking thicker and thicker until she felt she was suffocating under a physical weight. And suddenly the sword was speaking inside her head. *I'm sorry*, the voice said. *I can't . . . Oh . . . so many! So many!*

Through her own fear and confusion, Elspeth was aware of a new emotion, keen as a knife-edge: *grief* ?

Edmund, Fritha and Cathbar had all vanished: there were just the whirling creatures, the whispered name and the weight of her own limbs . . . so heavy, suddenly, that she sank down to the ground, her eyes closing.

'*Opith ther!*'

It was a woman's voice, low and commanding. The whirling spirits rose and dispersed at the order; spinning back to the cavern walls, writhing over and through each other in their haste to be gone. Elspeth blinked as the last of them vanished into the rock, leaving nothing but an empty chamber, quiet and dimly lit. The sword faded again as Edmund ran to her and helped her up. Fritha was sobbing quietly, leaning against Cathbar, but she seemed to be unhurt.

'You are strangers here, I see.'

Elspeth looked up speechlessly at their rescuer. A tall woman was standing in an opening at the far end of the cavern, smiling and holding out a hand in welcome. Her pale grey robe fell to her feet, and her dark hair was plaited and wound in a coronet on her head. She might have been a thane's wife at home, offering hospitality to guests. But what made both Elspeth and Edmund gasp was that she spoke in their own language.

'So few visitors come here, not all of us know how to make them welcome.' Her low, musical voice was warm, and she smiled at them ruefully. 'I am sorry that the spirits attacked you; they won't harm you now. Please, let me make amends: come and eat with me. It would be pleasant to have company.'

CHAPTER TWELVE

I found a mountain cave to be my forge, where fire burned beneath the ground.

There was a glacier close by, and at its foot a frozen lake. I saw movement beneath the ice: eyes and mouths and hands beckoning me. The voices called me to join them, become part of the ice; and I was kneeling on the surface, about to break through, when hands pulled me back. My son had come after me, and Ioneth.

She told me the creatures were the spirits of men trapped beneath the ice by Loki, left with just enough life to hunger and pine. Such spirits are everywhere, she said. From the sadness in her voice, I guessed her people to be among them.

Cluaran's horse was a good one, and the sharp-tasting air of the forest raised his spirits after the oppression of Erlingr's council. And though that council had wasted valuable time, it would be good to have Ari with him when he reached his destination.

'Nothing like woodland air to keep a man awake,' he called to Ari as they cantered between the thick trunks, 'even if this benighted land does produce nothing but pines.'

Ari merely nodded, urging his own horse to go faster. The pale man had been more silent than usual since they left the council chamber, and Cluaran wondered if he was already regretting his offer of help. No matter: like most of his people, Ari would keep his word, once given.

They left the forest a few leagues to the east of the lakes, so that they could approach at a gallop: the snow fields here were covered in grass in the summer, Ari said, and for a moment Cluaran pictured it purple and yellow with flowers and loud with insects. He had never seen this land when it was not under snow – except for the one time when everything was burning. *That will not happen again*, he vowed.

The lake shore was unusually silent as they approached. Some of the fishermen's tents stood in their usual places, but there were no fires lit, and most strangely, no men fishing, though it was the middle of the day.

'Something is wrong here,' Ari said.

They led the horses for the last hundred feet, and looked around the deserted camp, Cluaran checking the fishermen's tents while Ari scouted along the edge of the frozen lake. Cluaran had been through half-a-dozen door-flaps and discovered only that their owners had left in too much of a hurry to take their bedding, when he heard Ari shouting his name.

'Over here,' the pale man called. 'Something happened at this spot.' He showed Cluaran a confused mass of footprints at the lake's verge. 'See: three men came from the camp and stopped here, and met a single person coming from the other direction – someone with much smaller feet. There was a scuffle here; I would say a fight. And then . . .' Cluaran had already seen what Ari was pointing at: a jagged hole in the ice, much larger and more irregular than the fishing holes. 'Someone fell through.'

Cluaran was silent for a long time, pushing down the fear that grew in him and wondering if Ari would let him take the next step. But he had to find out. 'I'll call up one of the lake spirits,' he said at last. 'If someone fell in they'll know what happened – and whether he's still there.'

Ari had stepped back with a look of horror. 'You'll not speak to those creatures!'

'I will, if they have information for me.'

'But they're monsters – eaters of their own kind!' Ari's face twisted in disgust.

'You mean they used to be people of the Ice once, like you – before the Chained One took hold of them?' Cluaran spoke gently, but Ari turned his back on him and stalked off, back to the horses. Cluaran sighed and felt in his belt for his knife. He cut his arm, let three drops of blood fall into the water in the jagged ice hole, and stepped smartly back.

There was a boiling in the water, and cloudy shapes writhed about the surface. Cluaran leant forward so that his cut arm extended over the water, and waited. Presently a thin, greenish arm snaked out of the hole and groped towards his feet; then another. He kept well out of their reach and after a while they both retreated into the pool.

'Come on!' Cluaran muttered. He shook his arm so that another drop of blood fell – and before it could hit the surface a skinny figure shot out of the water and lunged straight at him.

Cluaran was ready for it. He grabbed the creature with his free hand and hauled it out of the water, holding it down on the ice as it struggled ferociously. The thing was slimy and almost without substance, slipping through his hands like waterweed, but Cluaran gripped it by the neck and waist and held on. Eventually it subsided, gasping.

'What do you want?' it asked sullenly, the voice bubbling in its throat. 'I will die if I'm kept out here – let me go back!'

'Oh, I will,' Cluaran assured it, 'as soon as you've answered my questions. And I'll reward true answers with blood.'

The water spirit opened huge green eyes. 'What questions?'

It took a long time to get all the answers he needed, and even with a dozen drops of blood, the creature was weak and half-dry when it had finished. It glared at him when he finally released it, slipping back into the lake with a loud splash which told him how much substance his blood had given it. Cluaran bound up his arm and pulled his cloak over it before he went to the horses: Ari would not want to know those details. The pale man was still scowling, his lips thin with dis-approval, but he listened to the minstrel's news.

'A human man and girl fell in the water just before sunset yesterday,' Cluaran told him. 'For a wonder, both escaped drowning. And the girl, the spirits said, was accompanied by Ioneth.'

Ari's eyes blazed, and for a moment the two men looked at each other in silence.

'The girl and some others were threatened by the fisher-men and fled from them across the ice,' Cluaran continued. 'They went in the direction of *Eigg Loki* and began to climb the mountain. The bandits who camp there followed them, climbing up the same path that the girl took. And later that night, the mountain was attacked by a blue dragon.'

'*Kvöl-dreki*,' muttered Ari.

'It seems so,' Cluaran agreed. 'So, by whatever bad counsel or mischance, it seems they are at the mountain after all – and the dragon-sender knows they are there.'

'We must go at once!' Ari cried. 'They're nearly a day ahead of us – he may have them already.'

Cluaran smiled tightly. 'Those were my thoughts as well,' he said. 'Except that he does not have the sword.'

'How can you know that?' Ari asked him as they mounted their horses and set off at a gallop around the lake.

'Because the mountain is not yet burning!' Cluaran threw back over his shoulder.

*

The sun was still high when they reached the ledge that led into the mountainside. Their horses had baulked at the bottom of the path and had to be left at the mountain's foot, but both men had gone that way before, and the climb was soon done. Ari shook his head at the signs of the dragon's attack: a dropped knife, a few torn strips of cloth caught on the rocks; and higher up, a patch of blood frozen on the stones. The ledge, when they neared it, was blocked by a great chunk of ice fallen from the glacier above, covering the dark crack that led into the mountain.

'They're inside,' Cluaran said. 'That path was not blocked by accident. Ari, do you know of another way in?'

Ari was already starting down the track. 'To the west; around the other side of the glacier,' he called back. 'It's lower, and more dangerous: the tunnel leads to the dungeon levels, where the spirits are hungrier.'

'And I'm short of blood already,' Cluaran muttered, but only to himself. 'Lead the way!' he called. They could ride again: the horses were growing skittish, but they would probably carry them around the foot of *Eigg Loki*. It would be better, much better, to get there before dark. He bent all his thoughts on speeding the journey – it did no good to think about what they would find at the end of it.

CHAPTER THIRTEEN

Once I began work on the chains, I had neither eyes nor ears for anything else. Erlingr's men brought me wood, and made alliances with the Stone people of the inland mountains to find me the ores I needed.

My son and Ioneth brought me food: they were always together in those days. She would not let him venture too near the lake as it thawed, saying the spirits there would feed on his blood. When she was with Starling she never spoke of the sword, and I knew there was more for her in life than her dreams of sacrifice and revenge.

The ghost-things still swirled above them as they crossed the huge cavern to meet their rescuer. Edmund could feel the creatures hovering just over his head, whispering words that he could not make out, but at least they were no longer pulling at him. When they had surrounded him, drifting into his mouth and nose like sour-tasting fog, he had felt that they had hold of something inside him and were teasing it out like thread.

One of the creatures drifted in front of his face, and for a moment its pale eyes looked directly into his. Edmund shuddered as the words it was whispering sounded clearly in his ears: *Ripente . . . Ripente . . .*

What were these things? Why had they been so drawn to Elspeth? he wondered. What had happened to her in that instant when the press of the creatures had blotted her out from sight? When they flew up in a cloud at the sound of the woman's voice, Elspeth was on her knees, her eyes closed and face contorted as if in pain – but she seemed to have recovered, letting Edmund pull her to her feet. She walked slowly, though, holding herself upright as if with an effort.

'This way.' The dark-haired woman was waiting for them under an arched doorway carved out of the rock. The lighted torch she held cast a warm glow on her face as she gestured down the dark passageway. 'The spirits are hungry all the time, and they are drawn to warmth and light,' she told them. 'But they don't venture into the higher passages – and they know better than to harm my guests.'

'Who are you?' Edmund blurted out. 'Do you live here?'

The woman smiled at him. She was beautiful, Edmund thought: slender and hazel-eyed, like his mother, though narrower in the face. Her bearing was as elegant and straight-backed as that of a queen, and he wondered what she could be doing in this forsaken place.

'My name is Eolande,' she said. 'I am staying here a while, though it is not my home.' Her smile faded. 'But come with me; we can talk later.' She held out a hand to Fritha, who was white and shaking, and the fair girl went to her gratefully. The others followed, though Edmund saw Cathbar cast Eolande a look of deep suspicion before he took up his place at the rear.

The new passageway was black, without any of the cavern's greenish glow, and without the sword there was no light but the flicker of Eolande's torch ahead of them. Fritha walked silently beside the dark-haired woman. Edmund kept one hand on the cold stone of the wall and Elspeth, next to him, did the same on the other side. Now that the swarming spirits were behind them she seemed to have recovered her strength, but she stayed close to him as they walked, and he found her companionship comforting.

'What were those creatures doing to you?' he asked her, quietly. She did not answer for a moment, and he felt a stab of concern. It was only natural that she should look drawn and tired, but there was a distant look in her eyes too, as if nothing he said could quite reach her.

'Weighing me down,' Elspeth said at last, with a shiver. 'They were flocking all around me, and calling . . . But I'm better now. I'm glad Eolande came when she did.'

'We were lucky,' Edmund agreed. 'What do you think she is doing here, under the mountain?'

'I've no idea,' Elspeth said, but her voice was vague, and she was looking at her right hand again.

'The sword – is it . . . ?' Edmund began, without really knowing what he was going to ask. *Is it controlling you? What else will it make you do?* 'How is it?' he finished lamely.

Elspeth stiffened. 'What do you mean?' she said. 'It's fine.' She looked back at her hand. 'I know how to use it now,' she muttered.

The passageway sloped upwards, twisting and branching, so that once or twice they nearly lost sight of Eolande's torch. Edmund tried to work out how close they were to the surface. They must still be under the glacier, surely. There was ice on the walls and floor, and there seemed to be more light than there had been when they first entered the mountain – but that could just mean that his eyes had adjusted. His feet slipped on the icy floor, and he and Elspeth clung to the wall and to each other for balance.

Suddenly there was a pale glow of light ahead of them. Eolande led them into a chamber roofed and walled with ice, through which they could see the beginnings of daylight outside.

'This room was carved out of the glacier, many years ago,' she told them. 'We can rest here.'

Edmund saw that the chamber was furnished: a straw mat on the floor, a wide seat carved out of the rock to the side of the entrance, a large wooden chest and – incongruously in this rough-walled place – standing on the chest, a beautifully wrought bronze cup and platter. The workmanship was as fine as any he had seen in his father's hall, showing coiled dragons and graceful branches. Something about the design tugged at his memory.

'Elspeth, look!' he whispered, pointing. 'Wasn't there a carving like this on Cluaran's lute?'

Eolande had overheard him. 'Cluaran?' she echoed. There was a note of recognition in her voice when she spoke his name. She picked up the cup and turned it in her hands. 'My husband made these for me,' she said, tracing one of the engravings with a slender finger.

'Do you know Cluaran?' said Edmund. The minstrel had been a demanding companion on the road to Venta Bulgarum, even infuriating at times, but he had proved a good friend in the end, and it warmed Edmund to remember him in this cold place.

He was about to tell Eolande that he had seen Cluaran only days ago, and offer her some news of him, but she merely said, 'Yes, I know Cluaran,' in a tone that invited no further questions; then, with a sigh, she set aside the cup and knelt to open the chest.

Edmund realised how tired his legs were as he sank down beside Fritha and Elspeth on the rock bench. Fritha was still shivering, sitting upright on the edge of the seat as if it was impossible for her to relax. Edmund squeezed her arm. 'I think we're safe here,' he whispered. 'The spirits won't hurt us now Eolande's with us.'

Fritha flashed him a smile, and sat back a little. But Edmund was not sure how much he believed his comforting words. Eolande was very gracious – and a friend of Cluaran's, it seemed – but they still knew very little about her. How far would – or could – her protection extend?

Eolande brought them a sackcloth bag containing some sort of dried fruit, which she poured out on to the carved platter, turning away with a smile when Edmund tried to thank her. His stomach was growling, but Fritha seemed too nervous to reach for the food, and Elspeth was looking down at her hand again, absorbed in thoughts that Edmund could not share.

'Here – eat,' said Cathbar gruffly, lifting the platter and brandishing it at the three of them. Edmund was surprised at the concern in the captain's voice. 'Eat, all of you. You need to keep up your strength.'

Edmund ate gladly, and Fritha seemed as hungry as he was. But Elspeth raised a berry slowly to her mouth, and chewed as if she did not taste it. Eolande filled the great bronze cup with ice-cold water from a barrel in the corner of the chamber, and they passed it from one to another. There was no other seat, so Cathbar sat on his cloak while Eolande knelt on the straw mat, looking as much at ease as a lady at table.

The water seemed to revive Elspeth. She drank a great gulp of it, and her eyes seemed to come back into focus.

'Eolande,' she said, 'what were those things that attacked us?'

Eolande's face darkened. 'They are spirits – spirits of the Ice people,' she said.

Beside Edmund, Fritha's eyes widened in fear, and he felt her tense as the woman went on. 'They were killed by Loki – I think you must know that name?' Elspeth nodded. Edmund thought he heard Cathbar groan under his breath.

'This whole mountain is named for Loki, in memory of the destruction he wrought when he tried to bend the whole world to his will, and was bound in chains by the elder gods. But many do not know that Loki still lives beneath this mountain.'

Edmund felt his skin go cold. All Fritha's old tales were true! He realised that he had never really believed it – a demon-god who could control dragons; could send his will across the sea. Fritha was white-faced, clasping her hands as if to still their trembling. Cathbar's hand flew to his sword hilt. Only Elspeth had not moved. She nodded her head slightly, as if Eolande had only confirmed what she already knew. But her eyes were dark with fear, and her right hand clenched so hard that the knuckles were white.

'We know of Loki,' Edmund said, feeling that he spoke for all of them. 'And we've seen some of what he can do.' He thought of his uncle, Aelfred: always laughing; tall and confident in his boundless ambition. But Loki had found him somehow, and had turned him mad. 'He has power outside the mountain, hasn't he?' Edmund's voice caught in his throat.

Eolande nodded. 'He has long been able to send his will outside his prison. He makes slaves of men and beasts, and draws life from them as they serve him. There are more of them in the lower caves, and in the waters below the mountain, never dying, but never truly alive. They crave life, and will feed on travellers if they can.' Her face was bleak. 'But the spirits you met have never served Loki. They were once an army, sent here to destroy him.'

'An army!' Elspeth whispered.

Eolande turned to look at her. 'An army of the Ice people. Sons, and brothers, and husbands . . . all destroyed. All condemned to drift in the caves, in the cold, for as long as Loki lives.' Her voice had hardened, and she fixed Elspeth with such a glittering stare that for a moment Edmund was afraid of her.

'So – pardon me, lady – how comes it that *you* are safe here?' It was Cathbar, shifting his weight uncomfortably on the cold floor. Eolande seemed to come to herself again: her face relaxed and she smiled at Cathbar.

'A fair question. I have had the help of all those who came before me.' She stood to refill the water-cup, running her fingers gently over its carvings before she set it down between them.

'I first came to the Snowlands as a young wife, travelling with my husband, the blacksmith Brokk. I knew little of Loki then – but word came that he had burst his chains and was about to escape the mountain. He had already brought fire and destruction to this land, and would destroy the world if he were freed. All the peoples of the earth were uniting to contain him, and they needed the most skilful smith to forge chains that would hold him. That was my husband.' She stared at the carvings on the drinking cup for a moment. 'He made the chains, and he and I helped to bind Loki again.'

'You fought him yourself?' Edmund burst out. He could not imagine this gracious woman in combat with a demon.

'How did you do it?' demanded Elspeth at almost the same moment. Eolande turned a level stare on them both, and Edmund felt another momentary shiver of fear.

'I played a small part,' she said quietly. 'Many, many people died to fasten those chains. A few survived, with the help of spells and charms.' She raised one graceful arm to show a twisted bracelet, wood and metal. 'That was how we were able to attack him.'

'But nothing can stand against Loki!' Fritha's voice was full of shock, and she gazed at the flimsy-looking charm in disbelief.

Eolande nodded. 'It's a saying of the Elder Gods, isn't it?' she agreed. '*No single thing can harm Loki; no single thing can thwart him.* But we did not fight *singly*, you might say.'

She rose and walked to the translucent ice wall. The light was glowing gold outside. Eolande went on without looking at them. 'All the peoples of the earth came together to fight Loki that day, each bringing their own skills. Even some of the Fay left their woods and moors to join us. Their magic was strongest of all.'

Fritha's eyes had widened in horror at the mention of the

129

Fay, and Cathbar stiffened. 'You called on the uncanny ones – on sorcery!' he exclaimed.

Eolande whirled to face him. 'They offered their help.' Her voice had hardened again. 'How else could we have come into Loki's presence and lived?'

'Can you bring *me* close to him?' Elspeth demanded suddenly.

There was a silence. Edmund felt an icy shock as he looked at his friend's set face. After all that Eolande had said – a whole army killed – how could Elspeth think of confronting Loki? How could she survive, whatever the protection?

'You think you can fight him, do you?' Eolande said softly, the glitter returning to her eyes. 'I wonder if you understand the dangers, even now. There have been hotheads before – and all of them ended in the cavern of the ghosts.'

Elspeth's face was pale, but Edmund could see from the jut of her chin that she was not to be frightened off now. She flexed her fingers, and Edmund waited for the flash of light to spring out – but the sword did not appear.

'I believe I can kill him,' Elspeth said. 'I've come a long way for this.' Eolande was silent, her expression unreadable.

'If you won't help me,' Elspeth went on, 'I'll look for him myself.'

'No,' Eolande said. 'I will take you to him. I know the path that leads to his cave. I would not take it willingly, for all the protection I bear – but with my help, you may survive him.'

Edmund looked again at Elspeth's set face, knowing that there would be no arguing with her. Whatever happened, he would not let her go alone with Eolande. The woman had offered them hospitality and maybe protection – but something about her filled him with unease. He glanced at Cathbar, who was scowling. The captain held his gaze for an instant, and nodded.

'I hope you'll not mind leading three of us, lady,' he put in, clambering up. 'I go with the girl wherever she goes. And Edmund, here, will not leave her either.'

Elspeth was already on her feet. Edmund jumped up to stand beside her, pushing away his growing feeling of dread. Fritha was standing too, pulling up her fur hood.

'I will go as well,' she insisted.

Eolande looked at them all for a long moment. Then she inclined her head, gesturing towards the glowing ice wall. 'It's dawn,' she said. 'We can leave at once: it's a long climb down the mountain, and best if we get there in daylight.'

At the edge of the chamber there was a narrow crack where the ice did not quite meet the rock. Eolande gestured Elspeth to go through first. 'It's tight for a few steps only,' she promised, slipping through the gap after her.

Fritha and Edmund followed, and Edmund heard Cathbar puffing and muffling a curse as he pushed himself through at the back. They were wedged between the ice and the rock, in a space so narrow that Edmund's shoulders scraped the walls on each side and Cathbar, at the rear, had to turn sideways.

They edged forward in the steadily brightening light, and after a few paces the passage widened a little. Then Edmund heard Elspeth gasp, and the next moment, she and Eolande had disappeared from in front of them. He and Fritha pushed ahead into blinding sunlight.

They had emerged through a crack in the ice on to the glacier. A roughened, grey-white sheet of ice stretched all about them, soaring up at their backs into a pale blue, cloudless sky. The sun was behind them, but even so the light dazzled Edmund after the dimness of the chamber.

'Tread carefully,' Eolande called, her voice sounding high and thin in the clear air.

Blinking, Edmund looked at the ground. Smooth, sharp ice fell to a narrow ledge, almost like a path, just where they were standing. From the ledge the tumbled ice of the glacier swept down to the distant snow fields, lying in a sheet of pure white far below. Edmund stared at the scene, dizzied by the sudden sense of space around him. Beside him, Fritha was also blinking in the sunlight, turning her head as if to savour the air on her face. They rested like that for a moment, hearing Cathbar's hoarse cry of relief as he emerged behind them.

'Don't stop here!' he told them. 'Keep up with the others.'

Edmund saw that Eolande was already guiding Elspeth away along the ledge. He started after them, his feet crunching on the snow that covered the surface. The ice above him was folded and pitted, even jagged in places, and studded with grey rubble – but the ledge, extending across the glacier ahead as far as he could see, looked smooth under its snow covering. Edmund quickened his pace, and immediately turned his foot on a hidden rock. Cathbar and Fritha were a few paces behind him, and saw him stumble.

'I'm fine,' he said hastily, but he went on with more caution, feeling his way through the thin snow.

Elspeth was at the front of the party, moving carefully but surely along the ice track. Unexpectedly, it was Eolande who stumbled. She looked back as if to check where the rest of them were, staggered suddenly and flung out a hand against the sloping wall of ice at her back. A crack spread across the ice from her fingertips, racing up the wall above her head. Edmund, already leaping forward to offer his help, heard the creaking noise from several feet away. Next moment the crack was a foot wide, stretching down below Eolande's feet. Elspeth had turned at the sound and started back, shouting something he could not hear.

'Elspeth!' Edmund screamed.

He was running towards the gap now, careless of the treacherous surface, with Fritha and Cathbar pounding behind him. He heard Cathbar bellowing his name. And then there was a great, crunching groan as if the mountain itself were bellowing in pain, and the ice dropped away beneath his feet.

Fritha caught him under the arms and hauled him painfully up, his back scraping against the lip of the crevasse, his feet kicking at nothingness. Lumps of ice were breaking off on both sides of him and falling into the yawning gap, to shatter on grey rock or vanish into the invisible depths. He was still staring down at them when Cathbar dragged both him and Fritha away from the edge to sprawl on the path a few yards back. At last the hideous noise was stilled, and even the skittering of falling ice faded to nothing.

Edmund pulled himself up and edged forward again. 'Elspeth!' he yelled, his voice sounding so thin he wondered if she could even hear him. Elspeth was a distant figure on the far side of the crevasse. She was standing on the very edge, calling to him; her voice sounded urgent, but he could not make out the words.

'ELSPETH!' Cathbar roared behind him, making Edmund jump and setting off another small fall of ice. 'Wait for us, girl! We'll find a way around! Halfwit that I am!' he added in an undertone. 'I *knew* the woman wasn't to be trusted!'

Elspeth was still looking at them, but now Eolande took her arm and began talking earnestly to her, pointing outwards across the ice. *She's telling her not to wait*, Edmund realised, and he knew at once that Elspeth was in terrible danger. *How could Eolande have made the ground crack open?* He remembered the woman's still figure standing at the very edge of the crack as it spread; her calmness, as if she had always known what was going to happen. She had her arm around Elspeth's shoulders now, and Elspeth was waving to him, then turning to go on. He opened his mouth to yell, *No! Stop!* – and instead, almost without thinking, reached out for Eolande's eyes, as the woman bent protectively over his friend.

134

He could see nothing but whiteness, and feel only a whirling mist: neither thoughts nor vision to catch hold of. Alarmed, he drew back – to find that the small figure of Eolande had stopped and was staring back at him. For an instant he heard her cool voice in his head.

You can't do that to me, little boy.

Then both she and Elspeth were walking away from him, down the path. Neither looked back.

CHAPTER FOURTEEN

I finished the chains on a day of clear skies and sun. A shadow fell on the forge, and I looked up to see the three Fay who had sent me here.

– Where is the sword? they asked.

I told them I could not make it sharp enough: that I had forged these chains instead. I said nothing of Ioneth.

– The Ice people will help me to bind him, I said.

They looked at me in silence for a while.

– It may contain him, the tallest said, but his tone was doubtful.

– It will not, said another, a woman by her voice. But if he must make the attempt, we will help him. The time grows short.

Did we really have to leave them?

The doubt had been growing in Elspeth's mind ever since she and Eolande had set off, leaving Edmund, Fritha and Cathbar stranded on the far side of the crevasse, but Eolande had guided her onwards with an urgency which matched her own impatience. She looked back in vain for any trace of them. The ridge stretched out behind her, marked with two sets of footprints, the pitted, rock-strewn ice soaring above it and stretching away to the edge of sight. She could no longer see any sign of the crevasse, or of her companions. 'I hope they're safe,' she burst out. She only realised that she had spoken aloud when Eolande turned to look at her.

'Why would they not be?' The dark-haired woman's voice was calm. 'There's a clear path back to my chamber in the rock; the spirits won't trouble them now. And if they do choose to come after us . . . well, the girl who was with you, Fritha, has lived in these lands all her life. She'll know how to stay safe on the ice. And the man, your servant, did not look to me like one who takes unnecessary risks. But we have no time to wait for them.'

'He's not my servant!' Elspeth began, but Eolande was already moving away. The ridge had narrowed: a little way ahead of them it lost itself entirely in the shelves and folds of the ice below. The slope beneath them was shallower than before, and Eolande took her arm to guide her into one of the ice furrows.

'The ground will be rougher from now on,' she warned. 'We must go carefully, but we cannot lose speed. If you are to succeed, you will need to be at the foot of the mountain before midday . . . you and Ioneth.'

Elspeth stopped. 'You . . . you know that name?' She had heard it murmured by the creatures under the lake; hissed at her by the spirits that tried to suck her life away, but never spoken by another living being.

'Of course,' Eolande said. 'It is the name of the sword you bear, as you must know yourself.' She had not stopped walking, as if unwilling to lose even an instant.

Elspeth started after her again. 'So how do you –?' she began.

'I knew Ioneth when she was a living woman.'

An image flashed through Elspeth's mind: a young woman standing as still as stone in a fire-lit cave, determination on her face. She had caught hold of a sword blade, and had dissolved; melted into light. And the sword was left glowing white . . . *I saw her! Ioneth: the girl in the cave . . . and the man who made the sword.*

Eolande had quickened her pace, her eyes on the path ahead. 'She had no family,' she said. 'She was adopted as a child by Ingvald, a leader of the Ice people, and his wife. It was Ingvald and his three sons who helped my husband to bind the Destroyer. Brokk survived that day, but Ingvald and his sons were all killed.'

Elspeth thought she could hear the sword's voice in a low sob, almost at the edge of hearing; but she only had ears for Eolande's story.

'Ioneth was left to the care of her grandfather, the clan-leader Erlingr, but she spent most of her time after her father's death with me – and with Brokk. She would stand by his forge and watch him work. I grew to know her, or so I thought.'

They were making their way directly down the glacier now, still within the fold in the ice; their footing made easier by the stones and rubble studding the floor. But the channel narrowed until there was scarcely room for one foot in front of the other, and ahead of them, Elspeth saw, it closed entirely.

Eolande turned to the side of the ice channel, clambering up it and moving across the glacier towards a furrow further along. 'This way,' she called. She said nothing more while they picked their way across the slippery surface and lowered themselves into the next rock-strewn furrow.

'So what happened?' Elspeth demanded when impatience became too much for her.

Eolande turned to look at her. The dark-haired woman's face was suddenly wary, as if she feared she had said too much. But she answered after a moment, without slowing her steps. 'When Brokk came to the Snowlands, it was not only to remake Loki's chains. He was asked to forge a sword – a sword unlike any other – that could kill Loki if the need arose.'

Elspeth's hand began to throb. She hurried alongside Eolande, stumbling as she watched the dark woman's face rather than the path; afraid to miss a word of her story.

'And the need did arise. Loki was chained, but the land still burned, and the hungry spirits began to appear, in the crevasses and in the waters of the lake. But Brokk said the sword was not yet ready. He had been working on it for many months – for longer – but he said there was something lacking in it; that it would not work. And then Ioneth came to him. She said that the sword needed a living spirit if it was to kill Loki. And she offered herself.'

The throbbing in Elspeth's hand had become almost too painful to bear. 'And he said yes,' she murmured through clenched teeth. The whiteness all around her was blotted out for a moment by the vision of the red-lit cave; the slender woman with her arms outstretched, and the grey-bearded man . . . Brokk, the blacksmith.

'Was Brokk older than you?' she asked hesitantly. 'Grey-haired, with a lined face and brown eyes?'

Eolande stopped walking, and turned on Elspeth with something like anger in her face. 'Older?' she cried. 'No! How could you . . . ?' She strode off again, walking on in silence until Elspeth feared she had offended her, and began to stammer an apology.

'You could not know,' Eolande said shortly. Her voice sounded strained, and she did not turn to look at Elspeth. 'Brokk was younger than me.' She lapsed into silence again, and for a while Elspeth walked behind her uncomfortably, not wanting to speak.

But I have to know! If the sword . . . if Ioneth is mine now, surely I have a right to know about her? 'Please,' she said softly, after a pause, 'tell me what happened when the sword was forged.'

When Eolande turned to look at her, the tall woman's face was composed again. 'I was not there,' she said. 'Brokk took Ioneth to his forge in the mountains, and returned alone. He said that the sword was forged, and that Ioneth had given herself to its making. But there was no sword to see. Many of the Ice people said that he was lying, that he had failed, even that Ioneth had discovered his failure and that he had killed her. When Erlingr threatened him, he stood in front of all the people and stretched out his arm, calling on the name of Ioneth – and a dazzling light sprang from his hand. They believed him then. Soon afterwards he went to fight Loki, alone. I never saw him again.'

They went on in silence for a while. Elspeth felt she should say some words of sympathy for the woman's loss, but the words would not come, and Eolande had drawn ahead of her, moving tirelessly forward even when the channel dropped sharply, or a blockage of stones forced them to climb. As she followed, Elspeth was struck by a wave of exhaustion that made her stagger. *We can't go on much longer at this pace*, she thought, as she scrambled and slid down another steep drop. And then the ice levelled out around her, and they were standing on a plateau near the edge of the glacier. Eolande looked around her intently, as if to see how far they had come down the mountain.

The sun was rising high above them in a pale sky the colour of a robin's egg, and now that they were lower Elspeth could see the peak of *Eigg Loki* soaring above them, dazzling white against the blue. But below them, the ice seemed to go on for ever, separating into huge drifts and gullies before it merged with the snow fields below.

'We must hurry,' Eolande muttered, and took her arm. For an instant Elspeth felt the sword's power scorching through her from wrist to shoulder, but the pain died down at once, settling back to a dull throbbing as she followed Eolande down another gully, making for the glacier's edge.

Eolande slowed her pace a little, so that Elspeth could walk beside her. '*Eigg Loki* burned for three days,' she said, her voice very quiet. 'The mountain shook, and the entrance to Loki's prison was blocked by falling rocks and ice. There was no more fire in the land after that: the snows returned, and Brokk was honoured by some as the man who had subdued Loki – though others cursed him because he had led so many to their deaths. Neither he nor the sword was ever found. A party went in search for him, and found only the gauntlet that Brokk had forged to hold the sword, lying on the ground by the stonefall. It was locked in a chest, hidden and forgotten . . . until you came upon it.'

Visions of fire and flashing metal filled Elspeth's mind: the grey-haired man, striking once and falling, wrapped in flame; the same man, gazing in horror at the sword that had joined itself to his arm; the slender girl, smiling faintly as her body faded. And someone else. In her vision of the cave there had been a third person: a young man, whose face she had not seen. He had followed Ioneth and begged her not to sacrifice herself. *Take me instead!* he had pleaded. She wondered who he had been, and why Eolande had not mentioned him.

'Was there another man –' she asked, and stopped. They

had reached the edge of the glacier. They stood side by side on a shelf of ice, with rock showing beneath. Below them to the left, the ice swept downwards, its edges sculpted into strange whirls, peaks and clefts. To their right, the rock descended into a jumble of huge boulders. Eolande began lowering herself from the plateau down to the rock a few feet beneath, and Elspeth swung herself around to do the same. She could see right up the mountain now: the whole route they had taken. There was the ledge they had gone down at first, with a faint line along it marking their footprints, winding upwards to the black gash of the crevasse . . . and there, at the top of it, just where the crevasse narrowed to nothing, were three tiny figures.

'Oh, look!' she cried. 'They're coming after us! Eolande, we have to wait –'

She broke off as Eolande put a warning hand on her arm. The tall woman was looking up at a point above the three figures. Elspeth felt another stab of pain in her right arm, and this time the crystal sword leapt out – at the same moment as the sky went dark above them.

The dragon soared overhead, utterly silent. The edge of one wing glinted silver as it banked, and one huge eye glittered at her. For the rest, it was a blue-black shadow, cutting off the sun. Even at this distance, Elspeth could feel the malice in the black-streaked eye. *Let it not see them!* she prayed, and felt a moment's intense relief as the creature swooped over Edmund and the others without slowing.

Then the eye rolled towards her. The huge wings folded back, and the dragon was descending, with terrible speed.

Elspeth scrambled down until her feet were on solid rock, and raised both hands to hold the blazing sword over her head. As the dragon dived towards her she thrust violently upwards, and felt the sword's point jarring against scales.

Next moment, something rammed into the back of her fur jacket, and she felt herself lifted into the air. One of the talons on the creature's trailing foreleg must have hooked her clothes. She screamed, and flailed wildly with the sword as she was swept around in a great arc with the other taloned foot swinging towards her, claws open to clutch at her. Then it had her around the waist, arms still free but waving uselessly, while the sword flashed like a lantern in a storm.

The dragon swooped once more, sickeningly, to where Eolande stood rooted to the spot. As its free foot seized her, the woman folded up as if fainting. Elspeth writhed in the clawed grip, trying desperately to find something to hit, but the dragon held on to her. She heard its roar of triumph like thunder all around her – and then it was plummeting with her towards the foot of the mountain.

CHAPTER FIFTEEN

I was soon to see Loki's power. The snows were melting from the mountains, leaving the blackened scars of the demon's fires; but the glaciers remained. And suddenly the men we gathered to bind Loki had a closer threat to face: the mountains around *Eigg Loki* shook, and from the glaciers came dragons to harry us – white dragons, filling the sky with their wings.

– Loki has called them from the ice, said the Fay; but the beasts' teeth could still bite, and their claws draw blood. Their frozen breath felled even the Ice people, and neither their arrows, nor the Stone men's axes, nor the magics of the Fay, could quell the creatures.

Edmund hung on grimly as his foot slipped yet again. The rope securing him to Fritha tightened and she looked down with concern. He forced a smile and waved at her to go on, then went back to studying the ice for handholds, concentrating on not looking down.

It was Fritha who had argued for climbing up the ice, and rather to Edmund's surprise, Cathbar had agreed. Edmund had wanted to go down the mountain. 'The woman said this lair she's taking Elspeth to is lower down – and anyway, how could we find a way up that?' he had protested, sweeping an arm over the expanse of ice above them.

But Fritha had disagreed. The crevasse widened rapidly below them, she pointed out, stretching so far that they could not see where it ended, but it narrowed to a crack only a hundred yards above. She thought she could find a path up a little way back along the ledge. She rummaged in her pack for a rope, which she tied around her waist and Edmund's, and also produced a metal spike secured to a loop of leather and a bag of wooden pegs, both of which she clipped to her belt. The route upwards that she pointed out looked like any other stretch of ice to Edmund, but Cathbar had looked up at it from one side, then the other, and nodded. And Edmund had agreed to go with them, looking beyond the crevasse at the two tiny figures, now almost out of sight as they picked their way across the glacier below.

'Reach up here, by my foot,' Fritha called to him, returning his smile. 'You climb well.' She turned back to the ice face, carefully chipping out handholds and footholds with the metal spike. Edmund, grabbing the hold she had pointed out to him, wished he believed her. Below him Cathbar was climbing steadily, his movements sure and controlled. His face showed worry, but Edmund knew it was nothing to do

146

with the climb: the last time he had glanced back at him the captain had been looking down, watching the narrow ridge that Elspeth and Eolande had followed. They were no longer visible, but Cathbar had stared along the ridge as if he could still see them. At first Edmund had tried to follow the captain's gaze, but the white immensity below them was dizzying, and he quickly turned back to the mountain face.

He had tried again to use their eyes, both Eolande's and Elspeth's, with no more success than before. Elspeth's sight had always been closed to him: it seemed the sword made her impermeable. But he had never met another living being who could block his gift – except for another Ripente, Orgrim, who had been his uncle Aelfred. *Could Eolande be Ripente?* The touch of her mind had not felt like Orgrim's. He remembered his uncle's mocking laughter, seeping into his mind like mist, and shuddered, pushing the thought away.

Fritha had paused, hammering a peg into the ice with the end of the spike. Waiting below her, his face pressed sideways into the ice, Edmund wondered how much further they had to go. He could see the crevasse only a few feet away, narrower already, but still too wide to jump – and the very thought of launching himself over that dark abyss, with nothing but sheer ice beyond it, made him cling to the freezing surface beneath him. He could feel the cold seeping through his fur gloves, making his fingers stiff and clumsy. He tried to drive away thoughts of the distances below him; the black drop so close; how easy it would be to lose his hold. The rope holding him to Fritha seemed very thin – and if he were to fall, really fall, he would take her with him. He was glad when Fritha started upwards again, driving away all thoughts but the search for a firm foothold.

Slowly, the crevasse alongside them narrowed. Edmund reached the place where Fritha had hammered pegs into the ice, feeling a surge of reassurance as he grasped the rough wood of the first one. It felt solid and reliable amid the slippery ice – like a link with the ground, unreachably far below.

He was able to make faster progress after that. When the crevasse was no more than a foot-wide crack, Edmund looked up and saw what Fritha had been aiming for. Above her head, the ice jutted out in a shelf, and changed colour: greyish against the surrounding white. There was solid rock below the surface: this was where the crevasse came to an end.

'This part will be hard,' Fritha called down to him, 'but we can rest up here, I think, and then find a way down.'

It was harder than anything Edmund had yet done. Fritha had to loosen the rope while she hammered in her pegs, edge outwards and finally lean backwards to reach the lip of the shelf. Edmund held himself quite still, peppered with shards of ice from Fritha's hammering. His hands grew numb, and as he watched Fritha leaning herself almost horizontally over his head, he could not imagine himself doing the same. *What will I do? I'll be stuck here – can Cathbar climb past me? Can I even get down again?*

Fritha grasped the edge and hauled herself up in one

movement, disappearing. Then her head appeared over the edge of the shelf, flushed and triumphant.

'It will hold us all,' she told him. 'Come, Edmund!'

She gestured to him to climb on, but Edmund could not move. His foot was on a peg, firm and dependable. Above it was only a snag in the ice . . . he knew he would slip . . .

'Go on, lad,' came Cathbar's voice below him. 'Up to your right.'

Edmund glanced to the right: yes, Fritha had carved out a hole there that he could reach. He went up another two steps, till the lip of the shelf was over his head, and stretched an arm behind him to grab the edge. His arms were too short to reach it.

'Lean back!' Cathbar called. Fritha added something encouraging from just above him, but he could not see her now. There was nothing but grey-white ice above his head. How could he throw himself backwards? He pressed himself against the wall again, afraid to move a muscle. *I can't go up or down*, he thought. *How long before I fall?*

The rope around his waist was tugged gently, and Fritha's voice came to him again. 'Edmund – you can do it. To help Elspeth.'

Edmund reached up and backwards once more, and this time found one of Fritha's pegs. He grasped it, and without giving himself time to think, lunged back with his other arm. One foot came away from the ice wall, and he kicked forward, trying to gain a purchase. Then his flailing hand found the edge, and next moment he was grabbed by both arms and yanked outwards and upwards. He cracked his chin painfully on the shelf as Fritha hauled him on to it. For a while after that he just lay on his face until the world stopped spinning, grateful for the feel of a solid surface under him. Fritha sat beside him, her hand on his arm.

'Thank you,' he managed after a while. 'I thought I was going to fall.'

Fritha nodded gravely. 'It's hard if you haven't ever done it,' she agreed. 'But for Elspeth, you will do many things, no?'

Edmund sat up, feeling awkward. 'Well,' he said, 'Elspeth and I have been through a lot together . . . she's saved my life more than once. I've come to know her well, I think. I know she sometimes seems to think of nothing but that sword, but . . .' He tailed off. 'She's my friend,' he finished.

Fritha was looking at him solemnly; even with a trace of sadness, he thought. 'I would like to have a friend like that,' she said.

Cathbar pulled himself on to the shelf. 'I'm getting old!' the captain puffed as he sat heavily down beside them. 'But you did well, girl, finding that route. Now, how do we get down?'

Edmund looked around. The shelf extended for several feet along the mountainside before merging back into the ice sheet. From the top it was brilliantly white: snow had collected on it, and the sun had risen high enough to shine on them now that they were out of its shadow. They could see much more of the mountain from here, but Edmund was still unwilling to look down. Fritha, though, jumped to her feet and went to inspect the ice on the further side of the shelf, looking for possible routes.

'She'll find a way if anyone can,' Cathbar said, looking after her approvingly. 'If we're only in time,' he added in a lower voice.

'In time for what?' Edmund asked, but the captain shook his head.

'I don't know myself, lad. But I do know that woman wasn't telling us half of what she's doing here. I think she's one of the Fay – she has their look about her.'

'The Fay? You mean the magic people?' Edmund was confused. 'My mother used to tell me stories about them. Don't they need the woods and fields to survive? How could one of them live here?'

'Oh, they can go anywhere – places the rest of us can't even find,' Cathbar said. There was a note of unease in his voice. He stopped as Fritha came back to them, her face alight.

'I found them!' she exclaimed. 'Come and look!'

They followed her along the shelf and looked where she pointed. The sun was glaring off the ice, but they could make out the ledge they had been following with Eolande, winding down the side of the mountain past the crevasse. As it descended the ice around it grew rougher, rising about it in ridges until the path itself was lost. But among the ridges, only a little way further down, were two tiny figures, one in grey; a smaller one in brown. Their progress was slower now as they picked their way through the ice furrows.

'They're not so far,' Cathbar said, excitement rising in his voice. 'We can still get to them. Do you have a way down, Fritha?'

'I think so,' Fritha said, pointing. A sound stopped her: a distant thumping, regular and soft, but heavy, and growing stronger.

'Avalanche?' muttered Cathbar.

Fritha shook her head, but her face was suddenly pale. The noise grew louder, and now it had a new edge to it . . .

Edmund found himself at the very edge of the shelf, shouting down to Elspeth – screaming her name as if he could make her hear him. For an instant he almost thought she had: a spark of light blazed in the smaller figure's hand, and he knew that the sword had woken. At the same instant the sun was blotted out, and the dragon was above them.

Cathbar pulled him back so violently that he fell down in the snow. Fritha had already thrown herself down – but the dragon did not slow as it soared overhead. They felt the gale as the great wings flapped, once, twice; and then they were above the creature as it swooped down the mountainside. It struck once – and two tiny shapes were dangling from its claws.

Edmund reached out for the dragon's eyes. For a second he saw Elspeth's face, full of terror, the sword blazing uselessly in

152

her hand. *Let her go!* he screamed at it in his head. But behind the dragon's ferocity he felt something else: another mind, cool and full of power, guiding the creature downwards.

He blinked, and opened his eyes to see the dragon sweeping down to the very bottom of the mountain, where the ice rose in great sculptured shapes that hid even its bulk from sight. He strained his eyes after it, but it did not reappear.

'So it has a lair at the foot of the mountain.' Cathbar had already recovered himself: his face was grim with new purpose. 'Well, girl, you show me the way down. I've hurt this beast before; I can do it again.'

Fritha was crying. 'The dragon mountain! Why did we come here?' she wept, and added something else in her own language. Cathbar put his hand on her shoulder.

'That's foolishness, girl. Elspeth would have come here whether you brought her or not.'

Fritha scrubbed a hand over her eyes and knelt to gather her climbing tools. 'Come, then,' she said. 'The way is not straight – but I take you down, as fast as we can go.'

'No,' Edmund said.

The thought that had just come to him was so crazy that he almost lost courage as they turned to stare at him. 'Fritha,' he forced himself to go on. 'You called this a dragon mountain. So they definitely used to live here?'

'You heard her,' Cathbar snapped, as Fritha nodded. 'Now are we going to get moving?'

'No! It's too slow!' Edmund grabbed Fritha's arm. 'Are there *other* dragons here? If we can find one, I can make it fly us down there.'

Both Fritha and Cathbar looked at him in astonishment. At length Cathbar spoke, more gently than before. 'It's a brave thought, Edmund. But you're talking about a dragon, not a dog. Even if we could find one, we couldn't control it.'

He thinks I'm running mad, Edmund thought, looking at the captain's concerned face. *And maybe I am. But it's the best chance we have!*

'You're forgetting,' he told Cathbar. 'I am Ripente. I can control creatures through their eyes – and I've borrowed that dragon's eyes before.'

The captain hesitated. He still thought this was foolishness, Edmund could see – but maybe not madness.

'Listen to me, Cathbar!' he pleaded. 'I can't get through to Torment here. Someone else is controlling it – if not Loki, then one of his followers, like my uncle was once. But it shows that dragons *can* be controlled! If there's another dragon here – one that isn't being watched – I think I can reach it. We'd be down there in moments, and we could go wherever the blue dragon goes.'

There was a silence. Fritha broke it, her voice as small as a child's. 'There are no more here like that one. The rock dragons are few, and they live far from each other. But my mother told me a story . . . There were dragons once that came from the ice: many, many of them. They flew from *Eigg Loki*, and they returned here. She said that they sleep here, always, under the glacier. And one day, they will wake again.' She looked at Edmund, wide-eyed. 'There is a place on the mountain called *Dreka-minning* – the memory of dragons – where they flew back into the ice. My mother showed it to me.'

'Could you take us there?' Edmund asked, hardly trusting his voice. 'Quickly?'

Fritha nodded, already scanning the mountainside for a route.

Cathbar let out his breath in an explosive sigh. 'So it's both of you, is it? You mean to go dragon-hunting – to gamble on a children's tale, while Elspeth's in danger!'

Edmund turned on him, all his fear and desperation breaking out as fury. 'I care as much for her safety as you! How many children's tales have turned out to be true since we've come here? Ice spirits . . . a god under the mountain . . . why *shouldn't* Fritha be right about this dragon? And we've no *time*!'

Cathbar shot him an approving look. As Edmund subsided, out of breath, the captain clapped him on the shoulder.

'Then let's be off, lad. Of course, as your father's son, you could just have given me an order.' He turned to Fritha. 'Lead on, girl, and let's find this nest of dragons quickly. I hope you're right about it, for all our sakes.'

CHAPTER SIXTEEN

Even without a guiding spirit, the sword had a good blade. It gashed the scales of the dragons, and kept their claws from me – but they did not bleed, nor tire. And then I saw my wife. She has always had the gift of speaking to birds and beasts. She was calling: at first to the dragons, and when they would not hear her, to the birds of the forest. A cloud of them came – crows, doves, even starlings. They settled on the dragons, covering the scales with black and brown till the creatures crashed to the ground. And still my wife called: to the hawks and eagles, which flew like daggers at the dragons' eyes. The battle turned.

– You see! she said in triumph. You have no need of swords. The creatures of this land can protect it.

– And against fire? said one of the Fay.

Caught twice – like a fish in a pond! What kind of fighter do you think you are?

Elspeth's sword arm was free this time, but it did her no

good: the dragon had gripped her round the waist, face down, twisting and writhing like a fish in a gull's claws. And writhe as she might, flailing with the sword, she could find nothing to hit except the claw holding her. In her first terror and fury she had slashed at it, and gashed the surface, but the sword would cut no deeper: she guessed it would not allow her to harm herself, or perhaps would not let her fall here.

The white ground soared to meet her as the dragon swooped downwards. Eolande hung limply from the dragon's other foot, the foreleg that Cathbar had wounded before. The whole leg dangled lower than the one that held Elspeth, so that Eolande was almost dashed against the ice as their captor skimmed down the mountain. The woman's face was pale and her eyes were closed. Elspeth felt a stab of bitter guilt: this was not Eolande's battle. She had brought this fate on them both.

The dragon pulled itself up from its plunge, wheeling dizzyingly in the air so that they now faced the mountain. They were flying towards another crevasse – no, a deep rift in the rock itself, stretching down nearly to the mountain's foot. The creature brought its wings in close to its sides and began to glide down towards the opening.

This could be its lair, Elspeth thought. *Is it taking us back to eat us?* She fought down panic, concentrating on the sword in her hand and trying to picture herself stabbing the dragon as its jaws came down to bite, as Cathbar had done. But the creature could have eaten them on the mountainside, surely, or killed them to eat later. No: their captor must be serving someone else, just as it had been before, when it had snatched her and Edmund from Venta Bulgarum. It was taking them to its master. *To Loki*, she thought: who else could tame a dragon? And after all, she was to be brought to him, pinioned and helpless.

There was a rush of wind as the dragon unfolded its wings again. It brought them down with a crack like the breaking of tree trunks, pulling itself up in the air with a jolt. Elspeth looked down. Something was moving on the ground just below them, flowing up from the foot of the mountain and gathering in the dark opening to the rift. Living creatures, long-bodied and low to the ground, their coats a soft silver-grey against the snow.

Wolves. White wolves.

Eolande gave a low cry, and Elspeth saw that she had opened her eyes. The dark-haired woman gazed down at the wolves, her face eager and intent, her lips moving soundlessly. The animals had gathered in a tight pack, barring the entrance. Dozens of sets of yellow teeth were bared in snarls. The dragon might have been able to fly over them, but its wounded leg hung down too low: already those at the front of the pack were leaping up, and Eolande had disappeared among a flurry of white bodies.

'*No!*' Elspeth screamed. She tried to slash downwards at the wolves, but the foot that held her was still too high. The dragon beat its wings once more, throwing itself back into the air; some of the wolves lost their hold and fell to the ground, yelping, but three or four still held on to the great scaly fore-leg. Hanging in their midst, still gripped by the claw, Eolande seemed to be unwounded, though the dragon's black blood ran around her. It seemed a miracle to Elspeth, but she had no time to feel relief. The dragon was swooping down again, shooting a jet of blue flame at the wolves, who scattered around it as it made once more for the opening. Elspeth flinched as a ridge of stone flashed by, inches from her face – and then she was being carried through a dark tunnel, with a rocky floor beneath her and grey walls stretching up to either side. A sliver of blue sky was still visible far above.

Something hit her in the back. A wolf had thrown itself against the foreleg that held her, and now it hung above her, growling, jaws clenched in the dragon's scaly skin as its hind legs scrabbled on Elspeth's back. She flinched as another wolf flung itself towards her face, its jaws dripping – but its yellow teeth clashed shut above her head, in the flesh of the dragon's foot. They were attacking the dragon, not her! A clawed foot scraped through her hair. She held the sword still by her side as more of the beasts leapt, caught, and tried to scramble up her body.

Through the press of rank, furry bodies, Elspeth glimpsed the dragon's other leg, still dangling low. The claw was empty. Eolande was free! But she could not see her companion, and the dragon was still gliding down the tunnel taking her and the wolves with it, wings swept back, unable to flap or to turn. It tried to flap once, the crack of air buffeting Elspeth's face, but the passage was too narrow to allow the creature to stretch its wings out fully, and it could not turn. It swept on, driven by its own momentum; neither the wolves' bites nor Elspeth's struggles seeming to slow it at all.

And then a shudder went through the claw that held her. Elspeth felt the grip around her waist slipping until she was held under her arms, her feet dangling. Next moment, her feet jarred painfully on stone. With a roar that brought fragments of stone down around them like rain, the dragon loosed its hold, sending her crashing down on to the rocky floor, with the wolves in a snarling, snapping heap on top of her.

The wolves' hot breath steamed around her as she watched the dragon retreating. In a few heartbeats it had reached the tunnel's end. The stone floor suddenly stopped; the dragon swept out into empty space; and the great wings unfurled. In the dim light that filtered down, Elspeth saw its scaly tail lashing and the empty talons dangling, one lower than the other. A single wolf was still clinging to the foreleg that had grasped Elspeth; one flap of the wings dislodged the beast and it fell, howling into the emptiness below. Then the dragon was lost in darkness, flapping slowly away into the void at the heart of the mountain.

The wolves had separated and were milling about her now, tongues lolling; their snarls giving way to panting. They seemed to be ignoring Elspeth, for the moment. But she had seen what those yellow teeth could do to a dragon's skin.

Moving slowly, trying to ignore her bruised limbs, she pulled herself up into a crouch, holding the sword at the ready.

A low, sweet whistle sounded behind her, and the wolves, as one beast, turned their heads to the sound. Eolande was walking towards her from the tunnel's entrance. The woman held herself stiffly, as if she had been bruised by the fall, and her grey dress was ripped at the hem, but there was no mark on her skin, and her expression was as calm as ever.

'They will not hurt you,' she told Elspeth. The wolves bounded towards her, surrounding her in a sea of white fur, and she stroked their heads and murmured to them as if they were hounds. 'Two of them died to save us,' she said, and her voice held real sorrow. 'But they will be avenged. Come.' She gestured towards the tunnel's entrance as Elspeth climbed to her feet. 'It's not safe here.'

She turned and led the way back down the tunnel, the wolves padding at her heels like lapdogs. Elspeth followed at a little distance, her mind racing. Edmund had spoken of strange wolves in the forest, on the journey from Fritha's home to the ice fields: creatures that followed them without threatening; just watching them. Were these the same wolves – and had they been following her all this time?

There was sunlight ahead. They were back at the opening of the rift, where the wolves had first attacked Torment. The uneven rock floor gave way to a jumble of huge boulders, stretching out to one side as far as they could see, and as far down as the snow fields below them. To the other side the ice rose in fantastically shaped ridges, tall as trees. The rocks immediately below them were scorched, and stained with blood. One dead wolf lay there, its fur white against the grey rock. Eolande stooped to lay her hand on its head and murmur something, her eyes sorrowful. Then she whistled again, clear and piercing, and threw one arm outwards. The surviving wolves streamed off in the direction of her pointed hand, leaping easily between the jagged boulders. Eolande watched them go for a moment, then turned to Elspeth, gesturing her to follow.

'Wait,' Elspeth said. Were they to go on without a word of explanation? 'Why did those wolves save us? Did you call them? And where are you taking me?'

'I am taking you to Loki's cave,' Eolande replied. Her voice was sharp, and she stood poised at the edge of a boulder as if impatient of the slightest delay. 'So was the dragon – but if you had met Loki in his claws, you would not have survived.' She reached out a hand to draw Elspeth towards her. 'Come with me, before he returns!'

Go, the sword said in Elspeth's head. Her whole arm jarred at Eolande's touch – as it had done when the woman grasped her arm on the mountain, before the dragon took them – but she nodded, and let the woman lead her towards the ice ridges, back to the edge of the glacier. She could feel the sword's voice murmuring uneasily – something was not right here. But the urgency was as great as ever, the voice told her, and the danger too. *Into the mountain – go!*

It was not so much a walk, Elspeth thought, as a battle with rocks and ice. They clambered over rough boulders and squeezed between the ones too tall to climb, their feet sliding on ice underfoot. Elspeth's hands were soon covered with cuts and grazes. She fell once, throwing out her left hand to save herself, and gashed her arm on a knife-edged snag in the rock. Eolande pressed on, hardly looking back, but Elspeth went more cautiously after that: whatever happened, she must not damage her right arm.

After a while they found themselves walking between walls of ice, towering over their heads. The ground grew smoother underfoot as the path rose, and Elspeth found herself sliding uncontrollably with every step.

'We are close,' Eolande told her, turning as Elspeth stumbled and clutched at the ice wall. The expression on the dark woman's face startled Elspeth: for a single instant she saw a blaze of urgency there that rivalled her own. Then Eolande turned abruptly and strode forward again, so rapidly that Elspeth almost had to run to catch up. How did she keep her balance? Elspeth tried to follow in her footsteps, and found that the going was easier: Eolande seemed to see all the places where the ice was rougher, or where near-invisible stones broke the surface. Either the woman had very good eyesight, or she had been here often.

But why should Eolande be so eager to take her to Loki? Elspeth wondered what else her guide had not told her. Were there dangers that she was concealing?

No matter, came the sword's voice. *Go on!*

And Elspeth pushed herself to go faster, keeping pace with Eolande. Her legs were trembling with effort and tiredness when the woman finally led her around a curve in the ice wall to meet a wall of rock. Overhead, ice met rock to cut off the blue sky. Eolande stopped, looking Elspeth full in the face.

'We can rest here for a while,' she said. 'I will answer your questions before I take you further. For the truth is, Elspeth, it is I who owe you gratitude, for coming here and for bringing Ioneth.'

She smiled – and Elspeth was suddenly filled with uneasiness. *Don't stop!* cried the sword's voice. *Don't let her explain! She must take us to Loki at once!* They were close to him now: Elspeth could feel it, like a dark undertow drawing her in.

No, Elspeth told the voice in her head. *I must know what this woman wants before I follow her.* The sword's pull was an almost physical force, but she set her back against the stone wall and listened to Eolande.

'First, I should tell you what I concealed from you before,' the woman said. 'I am one of the Fay. It is my own magic that protects me here – and will protect you too, if you go into Loki's cave.'

Elspeth's skin prickled. She had shivered when Eolande had first mentioned the Fay in her chamber under the ice: the uncanny people, who never allowed themselves to be seen by mortal men and women, though there were stories of them stealing away children. She had thought they were mere fables once – but then, she had thought the same about dragons and spirits.

'I thought the Fay lived in another world,' she said. 'The stories say they can't survive away from their own lands. How could you stay here?'

'It is hard,' Eolande said, and for the first time her face looked tired. 'The rest of my people returned to their woods and moors when Loki was bound again. I stayed because I had to. I visit the woods when I can; and the creatures of the wood, the white wolves, help me. I help them find food and protection, and in return they act as my eyes and ears. It was I who called them to save us from the dragon: if we had reached Loki still pinioned in those claws, you could not have fought him.'

'You sent the wolves to watch us, didn't you?' Elspeth said slowly. 'When we were still in the forest.'

Eolande nodded.

'Why?' Elspeth persisted. 'Why did you want to protect us?'

'Because I had long been looking for you – or hoping for you, at least.' Eolande's voice was suddenly unsteady. 'When . . . when Brokk disappeared, the sword vanished with him: we found nothing but the silver gauntlet. But he had told me what to do if this should happen. We were to lock the gauntlet in a wooden chest that he had made and keep it safe. There was a charm hewn into the wood that if Loki should ever regain his power, the sword would return. When Loki began to reach out and find himself servants, we sent the chest to my homeland for safe keeping. But still his power grew. And last year, he opened that cleft in the rock, so the dragon could fly in to him.'

She took Elspeth by the shoulders, staring intently into her face. 'Then the wolves told me that the dragon had brought a girl bearing a sword of light – that she had escaped, and was wandering in the forest. Can you doubt that I gave them orders to watch over you and keep you from harm; to bring you here if they could? But you came here on your own.' Her eyes were bright now. 'Ioneth had told you already what you had to do.'

They're so sure of me! Elspeth thought, not knowing if she was glad or angry or just afraid to see Eolande's confidence in her. *She's so certain that the sword . . . Ioneth . . . has made me do everything!*

But hasn't she? How much of this journey was my own choice?

To change the subject, she said, 'Why didn't you tell us this when you found us beneath the ice?'

Eolande looked abashed. 'Because the man with you, Cathbar, looked at me with such suspicion. I know the men of your country, Elspeth: they seldom trust strangers, and they are afraid of magic. I thought that if he knew I was of another race – that I was Fay – he would persuade you to have nothing to do with me. And I could not allow that to happen!'

'No . . . I see that,' Elspeth murmured. In her mind's eye,

she was seeing the blaze of the sword as it told her to block the path into the mountain, leaving Cathbar to the men who wanted to murder them all: *We cannot allow them to follow!* She felt a rush of relief that her friends were no longer with her: at least they could not be sacrificed to Ioneth's mission. She wondered briefly if the sword would sacrifice her, if it came to it. And she felt again the dark current, pulling her towards the heart of the mountain.

'I'll help you,' she said. Her mouth was dry, and the words came out more softly than she had intended. But Eolande heard her.

'The entrance is here,' she said, walking only a few steps further and gesturing to the rock wall. The outcrop of stone against which Elspeth had been leaning masked a narrow opening, so well hidden that she had to peer behind the stone slab to see the gap between it and the mountain wall.

'The cleft in the mountain, where the dragon flew, leads straight to Loki's prison,' Eolande told her. 'This tunnel is a longer way, but will take us there more safely – at least the dragon cannot follow us here. And you go in of your own free will; not as a captive.'

She stood by the narrow entrance. It was pitch-dark inside, and for a moment Elspeth had the feeling that the darkness was seeping out around her.

'We cannot take Loki by surprise,' Eolande said. 'He will know we are coming, and he'll throw up defences against us. Don't be afraid, Elspeth: it will all be illusion, however real it feels. He has no power against the sword, not unless you let him touch you. So keep back until you can strike cleanly. Are you ready?'

No, Elspeth thought. 'I think so,' she said.

She called the sword to her hand, feeling a thrill of fear as it blazed out. *Ioneth*, she said, *this is what you wanted. Don't fail me.*

I will not fail again! cried the voice in her head, fierce as fire.

Elspeth reached her sword arm through the crack in the rock, and forced her body after it, into the darkness.

CHAPTER SEVENTEEN

It took the skill of all the peoples together – the Stone and Ice people, the Fay – to return the dragons to the ice. One by one, they hovered over the peak, their breath foaming around them; then their wings folded back and they plummeted into the mountain. As each one crashed, a glittering cloud of shards shot up, hiding them from view – and when it cleared, there was only the glacier.

– But Loki is still unbound, the Fay said.

And, as if in reply, the mountain groaned, and a livid light shone from every crack and cave, as if its whole stony heart were aflame.

The sun had risen to nearly overhead, and for the first time since setting out on the journey Edmund found he was sweating inside his heavy fur cloak. Fritha had led them to a track that climbed upwards in a wide curve, with a stony ridge running alongside it to their left; Fritha often ran a hand along it as they walked, as if for reassurance. The snow fields were far below them now: when Edmund looked down he saw only a jagged confusion of ice and grey rock, rising to the next peak in the range. Behind that peak, rising sharp and clear in the hard light, the sky was a deeper blue than he had ever seen – but ahead of them there was no sky, just the grey-white surface of the ice and the ridge that loomed over them.

The surface was becoming smoother as they climbed, and Edmund's feet, which had grown accustomed to the rough ice further down the mountain, were starting to slip again. A couple of times Cathbar had had to give him a steadying hand – he looked over at the captain, trudging stolidly beside him, with a mixture of gratitude and shame. Neither Cathbar nor Fritha seemed to tire at all. Edmund's legs were beginning to shake with weariness, but he told himself sternly to ignore it: there was no time for tiredness. Elspeth was still in danger – maybe already in Torment's cave – and they were still on the mountainside far above her. They had to be able to fly down!

And what if you can't raise this dragon? a hard little voice asked inside his head. He pushed that aside, too. *I'll find it and raise it*, he told himself fiercely. *It will work. It must.*

'We're here,' Fritha announced.

She and Cathbar had drawn a little ahead of him. The ridge which had guided them this far had flattened out, and the two of them stood on an outcrop large enough to form a plateau on the mountainside. As Edmund hurried to join them he noticed that a dozen paces off to each side, the ice fell away sharply, the drop marked by two knife-edged creases of blue shadow. The plateau was like a lonely island in a sea of air.

Fritha and Cathbar were looking expectantly at him. *My turn now*, he thought, trying to ignore the sudden knotting in his stomach. 'Where is the dragon's cave?' he asked Fritha – and instantly saw dismay in her face.

'No one knows!' she faltered. 'I told you, no one has seen them; not in the memory of the oldest teller. All the tales and songs say they returned to the ice here, but no one has ever found a cave. Can you not call from here, to see if one will answer?'

'Of course – I'll try,' Edmund said hastily. Fritha's voice held more than a trace of panic, and he could feel the same fear beginning to squirm inside him. *No*, he told it firmly, and sat down on the ice, closing his eyes. Searching.

Cathbar's eyes, focused and intent, scanning the mountain ahead where the ice gave way to bare rock. Fritha's, looking anxiously down at him as he sat with his head bent. (*Am I really that puny-looking?*) He was crouched over, huddled in his furs, looking more like a beggar than a summoner of dragons. He straightened, casting his sight further afield . . . but there was nothing else.

He ranged still further. A bird of prey, soaring almost level with the peaks, its gaze on a patch of grey lichen on the mountainside . . . A small, vole-like creature, holding itself absolutely still in a rock crevice as it looked out at the sky.

Insects, scanning the pores of grey stone through multi-faceted eyes. Nothing big; nothing powerful.

He could feel the other two shifting uneasily beside him. In desperation, he cast his gaze downwards, to the foot of the mountain. Ah: something bigger; fierce, picking its way between icy boulders – wolves! He caught a flash of white fur – like the wolf whose eyes he had borrowed in the forest: but what would they be doing here? No time for that now . . . he probed further, into the depths of rock beneath his feet. Nothing but darkness. A faint impression of . . . something . . . might it be Eolande, who had the power to block him out? Or Elspeth, her eyes hidden from him by the sword? No, it was something else, something unknown. It showed him a glimpse of red firelight, the red of molten stone; fire reflected off iron . . .

There was a flash like lightning: cruel; burning with too much power for his head to hold it. *Laughing* . . . Then something slammed shut like a stone across a well, and he was lying on his back on the icy plateau, gazing into the dark-blue sky as if he might fall into it.

Cathbar and Fritha were leaning over him, talking to him, but for the moment he could neither hear nor speak. As Fritha knelt beside him and tried to raise his head on to her arm, her face twisted with worry, Cathbar's voice came to him, faintly at first and then more clearly.

'. . . should spread out; search for cracks in the ice. Maybe the boy will have more luck if we can find where one of them went in.'

Edmund wanted to shake his head, but he had no strength to move. He closed his eyes again . . .

. . . and it was all around him. *She* was all around him. He had been searching for a nest of dragons, packed together in a lair somewhere, like wolves. He would have picked out one pair of eyes, a single point of consciousness from among many. But this was no nest, and no single point. The ice pressing up against his body was part of her, but only a part. He had missed what had been there all the time. Something sprawled, dreaming, *huge* . . .

He jolted back to his own eyes. The dragon was underneath him; the icy landscape as far as he could see was all one frozen, scaly back. As his perspective shifted he saw the ridges of the spine, which they had used to guide their journey to this place . . . and beyond them, almost impossibly huge, the bulk of the enormous head: an ear-shaped scarp sloping down and down, smoothly, to the delicately curved cavern of a nostril. The folds of a wing stretched out to the side, extending further than his sight could carry.

He could not take her in. Like the mind amid the fire that had thrust him out before, she was too big; his head would not hold her for long. But Edmund had nudged her; shattered her unconsciousness. Cautiously, he reached out again and felt her stretching; the first stirrings of cool interest. But there was still nothing to see.

Open your eyes! he pleaded – and as if a door had been flung open, there was the mountainside: a huge swathe of it, covered in a strange, milky sheen like the thinnest layer of ice over water. He could see the mountain to the west, its snow still brilliant in the sun, and the top of his own mountain, too, the peak rising grey into the dark blue sky. The scene flickered sideways . . . and at the same instant the ground juddered beneath him.

Fritha gasped. Cathbar gave a bellow of amazement and grabbed her arm, dragging her down beside Edmund. They scrabbled for holds in the ice – suddenly moving beneath them as the dragon, with ponderous slowness, raised her great head and looked from side to side, lifting them high above the mountainside. A cracking and splintering filled his ears as all around them white scales burst through the ice – and beneath it all was the deep groan of shifting rock

'*Jokul-dreki*,' Fritha whispered. 'A dragon of the glacier! We are on her neck . . .'

'The whole time,' croaked Cathbar. 'And I thought I'd seen everything!' His stolid manner had vanished: he pulled himself to his knees and gazed around him with the excitement of a child.

Edmund tried to block them both out. The great dragon was aware of him, but not worried by his presence. He could not control her mind: it would be like trying to channel the sea, and if she wished she could cast him out like driftwood. *Please help us*, he tried – but there was only indifference in the vast mind.

And a flicker of curiosity. With a great cracking, one icy

shoulder peeled itself away from the rock, swinging the head around to take in a view of the ice fields below, soft white dappled with streaks of shadow, stretching unbroken to the vague mass of the forest far away on the horizon. He could feel the dragon's pleasure in the sight, but also her tiredness: she was so old; had slept so long. Did she really want to wake?

'Yes!' he hissed at her, speaking aloud in his urgency. 'It's important!'

He tried to nudge at the dragon's thoughts. There was an enemy at the mountain's foot, he told her: fly down! Attack! But there was no response at all. The long, slow unrolling of the dragon's thoughts washed over him: peace; sleepiness; the beauty of her home . . . and a vague irritation at the little gad-fly voice shrilling at the corner of her mind. No: there would be no commanding this dragon. Edmund thought of Elspeth, so far below, and wanted to cry out in frustration. *Edmund of Sussex – king to be*, he thought, *and I can't even order a dumb beast to fly!*

But a good king must know how to guide as well as command, his mother always said. Could he, perhaps, *persuade* the beast?

Edmund took a deep breath, pushing down his anxiety, and let himself share the old dragon's joy in the white snow fields, stretching beneath her from horizon to horizon. How wonderful it would be to soar over them, he thought, and he let his mind fill with the image: the freedom of it; the sun on his back; the wind washing over his scales . . . He felt the great body beneath him twitch in response. *Yes!* Riding the air, he

175

pursued; wings outstretched, swooping and wheeling. The head swung around again, and he heard a rush of air as the dragon breathed in – but still she did not move.

And then the dragon snorted with a sound like a storm-wind, and a cloud of shimmering ice motes fountained around her head. Next moment, Edmund felt the ground jolt beneath him, and heard Fritha cry out in alarm as everything around them shifted.

There was a creaking and cracking like an avalanche of worlds. They were raised suddenly, forty feet into the air, as the glacier dragon pulled one vast foreleg, then the other, free from the rock.

Edmund was flung back into his own sight like a fly twitched from a horse's flank. He crouched beside Fritha, blinking, as a folded-back wing lifted free beside them, sending cascades of rock and loose snow clattering down the slopes. The ridged back flexed as it began to uncurl from its long sleep. The dragon's body was too big for Edmund to take in the whole as it unfolded, but he could feel the gigantic creature stretch herself, shaking off the long stiffness, and feel the sudden surge of energy as she lumbered to her feet, took a dozen crashing steps up the mountainside and launched herself into the air with one thunderous beat of her wings.

The white dragon banked and soared downwards, swooping joyously over the snow plain. Edmund clambered to his hands and knees on cold, rough scales, peering about him through the whipping wind. The dragon seemed too huge a thing to be airborne, but she was floating like a feather, her shadow drifting along the snow below her. She wheeled, sending Edmund skidding along her icy neck – and he saw that Cathbar and Fritha had retreated along the great body to a hollow where the spine-ridge began. He crawled to join them, and the three of them held on to each other, pressing against the ridge and clutching at raised scales in the ice to hold themselves steady, while the glacier dragon celebrated her freedom.

'Well done, lad!' Cathbar shouted, over the roar of the wind. 'Now, can you get this creature to land?'

Edmund had been wondering the same thing. He reached for the dragon's eyes again, ice and rock wheeling dizzily around him. Before he could feel for her thoughts, a voice shouted into his ear, and something gripped his arm painfully. He jolted back to his own eyes to see Fritha's terrified face.

'*Kvöl-dreki!*' she was screaming. 'Edmund – he comes for us!'

Edmund looked where she was pointing. A black rift gaped in the mountainside below them, and from it the blue dragon was swooping towards them, claws outstretched. *It will take us as it took Elspeth!* was his first thought – but the dragon's master had no use for them: it was only the sword he wanted. So this was a quarrel between dragons, and Edmund and his companions mattered no more than trapped flies.

Torment's mouth was open, spitting gouts of flame as it came at them, and the black-streaked eye held nothing but death.

CHAPTER EIGHTEEN

We feared that Loki would next unleash a dragon of stone: *Kvöl-dreki*, or Torment, as he was known in our tongue. Most of our army would venture up *Eigg Loki* to try to stop the dragon before he flew.

I was to go into the fiery chamber inside the mountain where the demon was doing battle against his older bindings. Only a small force came with me: three men of the Ice people – the bravest, since they fear fire above all else; half a dozen of the Stone people; and the Fay themselves, my wife with them. Starling would not be left behind, and looking at his face, I saw how much he had changed from the laughing boy who had said those same words to me back in Hibernia.

The white dragon seemed not to notice their danger – or perhaps it was no danger to her, Edmund thought as Torment streaked towards them, wheeling in the air to attack her flank. She did not turn her head to the blue dragon, but Edmund felt the scales beneath him ripple as she brought her wings up, then down. The single wingbeat sent Torment toppling away through the sky.

'She is the whole glacier, this dragon,' Fritha said in wonder. 'She does not fear *Kvöl-dreki*!'

'But we still have to!' Edmund muttered. He pulled himself to his feet, looking back along the expanse of the glacier dragon's tail, to where Torment floundered in her wake. The blue dragon had almost been swatted back against the mountain, but it had pulled itself up, and was beating its own wings, climbing higher.

'Watch out!' Edmund cried. 'It's trying to fly above us!'

Cathbar, his boyish enthusiasm vanished as if it had never been, was already on his feet, his sword drawn. 'Behind me, both of you!' the captain snapped. Fritha obeyed, and knelt to get her bow from her pack. Edmund had no weapon – except that of a Ripente, the power of sight. He threw himself down to lie full-length, squeezed his eyes shut and focused again on the ice dragon's eyes.

Fly higher! he begged her. *This is your enemy!*

The dragon was aware of Torment's pursuit, but only as an irritation. She brought her head around to focus better on the approaching shape; wary but not fearful. Why should she be afraid of a creature so much smaller than she?

He is fire! Fire and destruction! Edmund insisted. He felt like a man on a mountain-top screaming into the wind. He could not awaken her fear. But there was anger now: *Jokul-dreki* had no love for fire. *Of course!* He conjured up flames in his mind, pouring out of the mountain over the white plain, boiling away the snow and turning the rock beneath to slag. He pictured Torment flying high above the desolation, bellowing his master's triumph – and he thrust the picture into the huge mind surrounding him.

A shock went through the ice dragon's body. She lifted her head and snorted like a warhorse, sending a jet of icy vapour down the length of her own side to engulf Torment as he rose above her. The blue dragon's flame died instantly, and he bucked in the air and shot away.

The battle was joined now. The white dragon was angry at being attacked; angrier still that this interloper would burn her beloved ice lands. But still she was bewildered: how could something like this happen?

Edmund summoned all his strength, calling up the memory of the burning thing that had mocked him and cast him out when he cast his sight under the mountain. *Loki*. A being all fire, all devastation; that wanted only to destroy. That could take your mind and twist it to his will . . . even the mind of a dragon as powerful as *Jokul-dreki*. He felt the ice dragon's furious outrage, and slid away from that thought. There was Torment, his jaws wide as the blue flame re-ignited, wheeling for another attack. Through the ice dragon's gaze the creature looked smaller, somehow. Lesser. *He is controlled by the fire-thing!* Edmund told her, and he felt *Jokul-dreki*'s belief, and her slow-burning rage.

He withdrew his eyes. Fritha was kneeling beside him, an arrow fitted to her bow, while Cathbar stood with his sword at the ready, holding on to the spine-ridge for support.

'She'll fight him,' Edmund told them. 'If she can stay above him, we only need to hold on.' They both nodded, but Fritha did not lower her bow.

And then the huge body beneath them gave a violent shudder. Torment was there – already attacking, darting his flame like an arrow into the hollow of *Jokul-dreki's* left shoulder. As she bucked in the air, and Edmund and his companions clutched desperately on to the ridge of her back, the blue dragon spat a second jet of flame at her. Torment was half her size, but he was much faster, and it was plain that his flames were hurting the glacier dragon. She did not roar, but snorted another great cloud of freezing air, while her front legs flailed at her attacker.

Torment dodged away, around the white dragon's side; for a long moment he was close enough for them to see his streaked eye glaring up at them. Then the blue dragon flapped to gain height, and the air was filled with the ripping-cloth sound of its wings. There was a whir as Fritha loosed her first arrow; it glanced harmlessly off the dragon's belly, but the girl was already fitting another, her hands quite steady. Cathbar was yelling defiance, lunging with his sword, but Torment was already out of his range.

As the dragon rose above them, Fritha shot again. The arrow rose straight and true, lodging in Torment's foreleg, but did not slow the beast as he swooped down on them, his mouth open to flare. But at that moment the great white dragon banked and soared upwards, catching Torment with the edge of a wing and knocking him away.

'He'll keep coming back, though,' said Cathbar grimly. 'And he only has to get us once.'

Edmund could see he was right. The glacier dragon was unwieldy, and slow after her long sleep. He could try to control her, make her outfly Torment, but he could not make her faster, or fiercer. Even as they watched, the blue dragon climbed in the sky again, this time from behind them, and began another long swoop downwards, jaws gaping around a jet of flame.

'Fritha,' he said quickly, 'give me one of your arrows.'

She held it out to him without question, and he rummaged at his belt for the cloth bag that Fritha's father had given him, filled with bread, at the start of the journey. It was coarsely made and too large for his purpose, but he managed to wrap it around the head of the arrow and tie it tightly with the bag's string.

'Can you still aim this?' he asked. She nodded calmly, and he was struck by her self-possession. She had thrown off her fear, focused entirely on the task in hand. *I hope I can do the same*, he thought – but by that time, he was already crawling down the ridge of the ice dragon's spine, towards their attacker.

Maybe seeing the blue dragon through the eyes of *Jokuldreki* had helped to conquer his fear of it, he thought. It was still terrible: the malice in the great eye as it bore down on him, the cruel talons and the fanged and flaming mouth; but the mere sight did not reduce him to helplessness as it had before. Even so, it took all his courage to stand there, unmoving, for the two heartbeats it took Torment to reach him. He waited until the dragon filled the sky ahead of him; until he could see the great nostril above him, taking in the air for the killing flame. Then he threw himself flat, pulling his heavy fur cloak over his head, while one gloved hand thrust the muffled arrow out and upwards.

He felt the *whoosh* as the flame rushed over him, and the clap of air as the dragon sailed overhead. He threw off the singed cloak and scrambled to his feet, holding the arrow carefully. The coarse material had caught the flame and was beginning to blaze up.

Torment was in the sky ahead of them, already turning for another attack. Cathbar had been swiping at the dragon each time it went over, ensuring that it could not come too low, but never landing a stroke. The captain stopped in mid-curse when he saw what Edmund was holding. Fritha, her face intent, had already taken up her position to fire again, holding out her hand for the arrow.

'Aim for the eye, girl!' Cathbar told her. He and Edmund crouched behind her, waiting in silence.

Torment was climbing, preparing for a swoop straight down. This time, the talons were extended: the dragon was intending to seize, or rend. And then Torment was dropping, the air screaming in his wake – and Fritha's blazing arrow was rising to meet him.

It caught Torment in his wounded eye. The dragon's shriek rocked them like a physical force; even the glacier dragon shuddered along her immense length to hear it. Then Torment was gone, falling from the sky like a stone.

Edmund lay flat on the ice dragon's back, looking only at the cold, pulsing scales by his head. His head ached with effort and tiredness, and any movement sent a fresh stab through it – but for the moment, there was time to rest. They had seen the blue dragon flap away, still screaming, to vanish into the cleft in the mountain from which he had first appeared, and *Jokul-dreki* was following him – at least, making for the outside of the ravine. Once there, they could follow the wounded dragon and – finally – find Elspeth.

The glacier dragon wheeled gently in the air and began a stately descent. Edmund reached for her eyes one last time, wondering how heavily she would land. He could see the mountains coming up at him from both sides and a huge arc of the sky above, but nothing directly below them. He wished she would bank a little, to show him the surface below, and to his surprise, the ice dragon obeyed. *Jokul-dreki* seemed willing to let him guide her now, after the encounter with Torment – or perhaps she was just weary again. Edmund himself had been too exhausted even to celebrate their victory, and he suspected his companions felt the same; though Cathbar, with rare expansiveness, had clapped each of them on the shoulder and called them a grand pair of fighters. Fritha had smiled at both of them, but had said very little. She sat beside Edmund now, still and silent, watching as he tried to steer their great mount safely to the ground.

Edmund called out a warning to hold on as he told the dragon to bank again. They needed to land at the edge of the snow field, far enough from the foot of *Eigg Loki* to touch down smoothly; close enough to reach the mountain as soon as they could. And after that . . . The ravine gaped ahead of them. They would have to climb up to it from the mountain's foot, but once there, it could not be too hard to track Torment back to his lair and rescue Elspeth. *If she's alive* . . . said the little voice in his head, but he pushed it away.

Through the white overlay of the dragon's vision he saw the tumbled boulders of the mountain's foot, and something else: horses? Two brown-clad horsemen were halted at the edge of the snow field, watching their descent. In his surprise he almost released the dragon's eyes: who were they? *Jokul-dreki* saw them just as interesting new creatures, neither welcome nor threatening, though he could feel the great creature angling her descent to avoid crushing them.

'Who are *they*?' Fritha murmured beside him. 'What do they do here?'

'Just as long as they're not more of those bandits.' Cathbar's voice was uneasy. 'Mind you,' he added, brightening, 'they're not likely to give us trouble, seeing what we're riding!'

There was a jarring thud, and for a few moments Edmund and Fritha were clutching each other, sprawled on the dragon's icy hide as her immense bulk ploughed through the snow surface and ground to a halt among the rocks. Behind them, Cathbar lay flat, clinging with both hands to the spine-ridge and breathing hard.

'It seems I'm not needed!' called a familiar voice below them. One of the men had dismounted and strode up to the dragon's foreleg, throwing back his hood. 'I travel hundreds of leagues to your rescue, and find you summoning dragons.'

It was Cluaran.

Edmund blinked, trying to accustom himself to his own eyes as the minstrel's face swam into his vision. Without the pearly colours of the dragon's vision, everything seemed too sharp and bright, and his ears were full of the grinding of her great belly on the rocks and the huge rush of icy air as she lowered and folded her wings. He took Cluaran's offered hand to lower himself shakily to the ground, and hugged the man impulsively. Whatever he had thought about him in the past, it was a joy to see the minstrel again, and to know that he and Elspeth had not been forgotten.

'Did you really come out here to find us? But how did you know where we would be?'

'It was always certain that the dragon would take you to *Eigg Loki*.' Cluaran's face was suddenly sombre. 'Ari, here, is of the Ice people; he helped me find the way,' he added. His companion put back his hood with a nod of greeting, revealing a face as pale as milk.

Edmund introduced Fritha as the minstrel helped her and Cathbar down. The fair-haired girl smiled at him in gratitude, but Edmund noticed that she drew back from Ari.

'Where is Elspeth?' Cluaran demanded. 'Is she not with you?'

Edmund's brief glow of joy vanished. 'Torment took her!' he burst out. 'That's why we're here; we think he has taken her to his cave.' He looked up at the cleft in the mountainside above them, black in the afternoon light. 'We flew the ice dragon down here, so that we could follow.'

Ari was looking at him with open wonder. 'You commanded *Jokul-dreki*!' the pale man exclaimed.

'I have to reach Elspeth,' Edmund said. The sense of urgency was gripping him again. He realised that he was swaying on his feet, and put a hand out to the ice dragon to steady himself. He must not weaken now! 'Cluaran; will you come with us?' he asked.

'We both will,' Cluaran said, looking at Ari. 'But not by that cave: it leads to a sheer drop. There is a tunnel, a longer but surer way in, not far from here. Come!'

He took his horse's rein and began to lead it along the foot of the mountain, beckoning to the rest of the party to follow. In spite of his haste, Edmund lingered a moment behind them, where the white dragon lay like a ridged hill in the snow. One huge, slanted eye opened to look at him, as green as glass and deep as the ocean.

'Thank you,' he said aloud, uncertain if she would understand him. *You're weary*, he told her in his mind; *so am I. But you can sleep now.*

The glacier dragon looked at him for a long moment; then the eye closed, and she was lost in the landscape; to all appearances just a hummock of ice. Edmund turned from her and ran after the others.

Cluaran tied the two horses in a cleft at the mountain's foot, and he and Ari found nosebags and blankets for them among their baggage. 'No water,' Cluaran said regretfully, 'but at least they'll be safe from Torment here. And now we must hurry.' He turned to Edmund. 'It was mid-morning when the dragon took her, you said?'

'The sun was just above the mountain-top,' Edmund told him, feeling afresh how long it had been. 'And she and Eolande were halfway down . . .'

Cluaran had laid a heavy hand on his arm. 'Who did you say was with Elspeth?' he interrupted. His voice was suddenly tense, and his eyes had hardened.

'Eolande,' Edmund stammered. 'A tall lady with dark hair. We met her inside the mountain; she said she knew you. She . . . she was leading us to Loki.' Beside him, Fritha was nodding.

Cluaran and Ari exchanged a glance; of alarm, Edmund thought. When Cluaran spoke again, his voice was tight with suppressed fury.

'Fool that I am!' he muttered. 'What has he done to her?'

He turned to the others. 'No time now. If I take you into the mountain, you must stay behind me and do as I say, do you hear? Even you, captain. Weapons are useless against Loki – all but one – and he is cunning. He'll turn your mind . . .' His voice broke, and he said no more. In silence, they followed him into the jumble of boulders at the mountain's foot.

As he scrambled over the rocks, Edmund wondered both at the minstrel's words and at his tone. What did Cluaran know about Eolande? Edmund already suspected that the woman was leading Elspeth into some danger. If only they had met up with Cluaran before: he might have warned them! But there was no time for questions now. Cluaran was leading them at a breathless pace, but it was not fast enough for Edmund.

She's still alive, he told himself fiercely. *She has to be. We'll find her soon . . . and whatever is in there with her, we'll save her.*

CHAPTER NINETEEN

When we entered the chamber, four of us fell before the Fay could shield us. They made us a bridge over a river of fire, and we crossed to the demon, a living, grinning flame.

My son caught Loki's right hand and chained it, while he flung screams at us like swords. I thrust a band around the monster's neck, and hammered both chains deep into the rock. And then we ran, back through the flames.

My wife was safe, and one of the Fay. One of the Ice men was clinging to my son, each keeping the other on his feet. All the rest were dead – but we believed we had triumphed. Then we discovered what had been done to the army above us.

The darkness surrounded Elspeth, following behind her and lying in wait for her at every step. She and the sword moved forward in a little ring of brightness which had nothing to illuminate – nothing but grey, featureless rock wall on each side. There was never anything ahead of her to throw back the light; not so much as a different colour in the rock or a turn in the path. There was no ice here: they were descending little by little into the depths below the mountain, and it was growing warmer. Elspeth's footsteps seemed muffled; Eolande's, behind her, could hardly be heard at all. And the tunnel seemed to go on for ever.

The sword's glow seemed to be getting brighter, hurting her eyes, though it still showed her nothing. Elspeth realised that the walls were closer than they had been – and there was stone over her head now, where before there had been nothing but blackness. A few more paces and the rock was pressing on her. The tunnel was moulding itself to her shape, so that every step meant pushing through stone. Her chest tightened and she felt her heart racing. *It's not real*, she told herself – but the rock was solid all around her, and it was getting harder to breathe.

Now two ridges formed on each side of her neck, forcing her head up so that she could not turn. She could feel the rock pushing against both sides of her arms. She had lost all sense of the sword in her hand: her body was hardening, becoming part of the stone . . .

'It is an illusion,' said Eolande's soft voice behind her. Elspeth forced her eyes open. She was standing rigidly in the middle of the tunnel, the sword stretched out ahead of her. The walls were as featureless as ever; the roof still lost in darkness over her head. Only her shoulders and legs were knotted in cramp. She took a ragged breath and walked on, her legs trembling as the cramp released her.

'Did you feel it too?' she demanded. 'The rock closing in?'

'Loki can force his visions on more than one at a time,' Eolande told her. 'Or attack just one among many. He will use your own fears, your own demons, to torment you.' She did not say anything about her own experience just now, and Elspeth found herself wondering whether this calm, poised woman *had* any fears of her own.

Elspeth was on her guard after that. Later – there was no way to tell how much later, or how far they had come – she noticed a change in the sound of their footsteps on the stone floor: they were softer, as though treading on earth . . . or through mud. The ground beneath her had grown yielding, sucking her feet into it with each step.

The walls were no longer stone but something wet and reddish, curving around her. It was a gullet, or a snake's belly; she felt the life pulsing through it and almost lost her footing, to be sucked down the tube and swallowed up. *It's illusion!* she told herself. *Just a lie to scare me!* – and she drove the sword hard into the slimy redness at her feet. The clang of metal on stone recalled her at once to the rock tunnel. She whirled to see Eolande close behind her: the Fay woman gave her an approving look, but said nothing. The sword throbbed in her hand: *Go on! We are close now!* Of course, Elspeth thought. The sword – Ioneth – could stand against Loki: even against his visions. She was the only thing more powerful than the demon-god, had given her own life to make the sword's blade so.

They went on in silence, and there were no more illusions. Elspeth found herself walking faster, as if that might make the distance shorter; Eolande matched her pace, staying always a few steps behind her. She could feel the sword constantly in her mind now: not Ioneth's voice, but a low, feverish thrumming almost at the edge of hearing, that built in intensity with every step.

The air grew steadily hotter, and Elspeth took off her fur cloak and carried it over her arm as she walked. She thought briefly of abandoning it, to retrieve later, but there was no certainty that they would leave the mountain by the same route. *We might never leave at all*. The words flashed through her head, leaving a cold wake – but she did not slow her steps. A sense of unreality had been growing in her: it was hard to imagine anything outside the tunnel, anything but this endless walk through grey stone, with blackness before and after.

When a point of red light appeared in the distance, Elspeth tensed, expecting some new trick. But the light stayed where it was, growing brighter as they approached and casting a dim glow on the walls to either side. The heat was becoming stifling, and Elspeth felt sweat running down her neck. The sword's hum had become a singing in her head, fierce and eager.

'We are almost there,' Eolande murmured, her soft voice making Elspeth jump. The Fay woman seemed as unaffected by the heat as she had been earlier by the cold. In the sword's white light her face was pale and calm, but a sudden eagerness flickered in her eyes.

Almost there, came Ioneth's voice, urgently, and Elspeth felt the dark undertow again, pulling her forward. The sword jumped in her hand – and a thrill of terror shot through her. In just a few moments, perhaps . . . She tried to push the thought away, reaching for the dreamlike unreality that had lain on her before, but it would not come. She stopped, her legs suddenly heavy. A wave of panic hit her. *I can't do this!*

It's just the wait that's bad. The not-knowing. Her father's voice came to her, back in her childhood, far from land on the *Spearwa* and facing her first ever storm. She had clung to him in panic as the black clouds rolled towards them. *Once the storm breaks, there's plenty to do; you'll have no time to be scared.* And he had been right. After the mad flurry of the storm he had hugged her fiercely: *my brave girl.* Through all the tempests they had faced together after that, she had never felt fear – not even on that last day, in the icy water.

Eolande was watching her, waiting patiently but with that same undercurrent of eagerness. Elspeth breathed deeply, flexed her arms and felt the weight of the sword in her hand. *Ioneth?* she called in her mind, and the sword throbbed in answer: *I am ready!*

Without giving herself more time to think, Elspeth strode towards the red light.

With something to focus on at the end of the tunnel, the way seemed short. The red glow grew stronger, rivalling the white light of the sword until they seemed to be walking into fire. The walls ahead of them gleamed and flickered with it.

Just before the walls gave way to open space, Eolande laid a hand on her shoulder.

'Remember – do not let him touch you!' she breathed. She looked as if she would have said more, but Elspeth nodded briefly and turned from her. It was too late for advice. She felt her heart beating in time with the pulsing of the sword as she stepped through the red-lit opening.

The cavern beyond was vast, bigger than any godshouse Elspeth had seen, even the one at Glastening. The rock walls, black rather than grey, stretched off into the distance to both sides and soared above her head into darkness. The red light came from a trench filled with fire, running along the far side of the cave, more than forty paces away. Flames leapt up from it, then died again, casting a flickering light on the figure that hung from the rock beyond.

A tall and muscular man hung limply from chains that bound him to the rock. Elspeth peered across the cave, but she could see no more through the leaping flames.

'The river of fire that you see is molten rock,' Eolande murmured. 'It would not hold him for an instant if he were free, but it stops people from coming to him when he catches their minds and calls them. Come – I can help you to cross it.'

The ground was rough and black, like cinders. Eolande led her across the vast empty space, the soft fall of their steps drowned out by the crackling of the fire. Elspeth's eyes were fixed on the hanging figure that flickered in and out of sight through the flames. She drew closer. So this was her enemy; the murderer of her father, and countless hundreds besides, now and a hundred years ago. He had destroyed everything she held dear; her whole past life. *And all my people, generations upon generations, all gone*, Ioneth said in her head. Her voice seemed to join with Elspeth's own. *Face me! I am here!*

But he was so still, so silent! He did not even seem aware of their presence. As she approached, she saw that he was fastened to the rock by five chains, from manacles on wrists, ankles and neck. His head was lowered, so she could not see his face. Close to his feet, the river of rock bubbled red and yellow, unbearably bright and sending out a fierce heat that made Elspeth shield her face with her hand. Flames danced on its sluggishly flowing surface.

Eolande had gathered a little heap of black stones, of the same material as the cindery ground. She threw one of them into the fiery river – Elspeth saw how it floated on the surface – and another, and another. When the bubbling surface was covered with black discs, she emptied a little phial into her hand and blew its contents over the rocks, then spoke in a language which Elspeth did not understand. There was a loud hissing, and a cloud of smoke rose from the river, pushing the flames aside. As it cleared, she saw that the black rocks had formed a bridge, narrow and fragile-looking but keeping the fire at bay, at least for the moment.

'Cross quickly,' Eolande told her. 'It will not last long.'

Elspeth set a cautious foot on the bridge. It seemed to bear her weight. She stepped on to the cindery surface, the blood singing in her ears, and walked forward. She felt the little bridge shaking as Eolande crossed behind her.

As she reached the far bank, the figure chained to the rock stirred for the first time, uttering a low sound like a groan or growl. He hung as if exhausted, his muscles straining against the bands that held him. His head was tipped forward as if it were too heavy for him to lift; Elspeth could see only a tangle of black hair. But as she approached, he spoke without raising his head, his voice low and hoarse:

'So you are here at last.'

The sword leapt in her hand in a blaze of white: *now!*

Elspeth walked forward steadily. Without willing it, she found her arm rising to strike. She could feel Eolande just behind her; feel the sword pulling her hand, both of them driving her on – as if she had no power over her own body. But her mind was still her own. This chained man before her, without even the strength to lift his head . . . how could he be a god? His bare arms were tanned and streaked with sweat, and he wore a rough tunic, much like those worn by the sailors at home.

I can't just kill him! she told the sword.

Now, now! the voice repeated. *Before he looks at you.*

Elspeth took another step forward. She was close enough to strike now: the sword vibrated in her hand, urging her arm forward. And the figure raised his head and smiled at her.

It was her father.

Her heart became a stone in her chest. She could not move, it was so heavy. Her body was ice. She stood, drinking in her father's face with a desperate hunger as he looked at her, smiling and then serious. *My girl, grown up so fine and brave . . .*

The sword was screaming in her mind, but she could not make out what it said. Then a cool hand touched her arm: Eolande. The Fay woman clasped Elspeth's sword hand in both of her own, and the blade writhed like a snake, its shrieks redoubling. But Eolande's voice, calm and reassuring, carried through it all.

'Don't fear, Elspeth. Let me help you.'

Her hands were cold and smooth as marble as she brought Elspeth's sword arm down.

CHAPTER TWENTY

They were all dead – every man. Their spirits wailed around us, trapped by the one we had chained below.

We took what we could find for burial, knowing we had failed. Loki was bound again – but too much had been lost.

Erlingr cast us out. His son and grandsons were dead, and all through my fault, he said.

And then Ioneth came to me.

– It's time to forge the sword, she said. We must kill him.

I looked around me, at the shattered men, the weeping women, and far off, the blackened mountain.

I could not refuse her.

The tunnel mouth was further along than Cluaran remembered, and when he did reach it he almost walked past the opening before he recognised the spot. *Careless!* he chided himself. *Keep your wits about you, man!* Eolande's name, so innocently mentioned by Edmund, had plunged him into confusion – but there was no time now for grief or guilt. *Think of that later – for now, you've work to do.*

He gathered the group about him. Ari knew the place nearly as well as he did; he would be a good ally here. But the humans . . . well at least he could put them on their guard.

'This passage leads to the cavern of Loki, under the mountain,' he told them. 'You should know that he is still powerful, though chained. He will sense us coming, and it amuses him to play tricks on his visitors. Captain Cathbar, and you, girl: there's no reason for you to come with us.' There was no reason for Edmund to accompany them either, he thought, but he knew better than to suggest that. The boy would not wait outside while Elspeth was in danger.

Cathbar flatly refused to stay outside, and so did the girl, to Cluaran's surprise. She was white in the face, but her expression was determined, and Cluaran was too full of haste to argue. He pulled a stick of firewood from his pack and began to wrap it in cloth for a makeshift torch while he gave his instructions.

'We'll have to go single file. Whatever you see, whatever you feel in the tunnel, do not run. Loki is the master of lies, remember that. He cannot harm you unless he touches you.'

They all nodded, and he gave them one last, doubtful look. The captain would obey orders, he knew – and the girl was doing a fair job of hiding her terror, though she was plainly nervous of Ari. *Grown up on tales of ice monsters, no doubt*, he thought wryly. As for Edmund, the boy was exhausted, but there was something new about him – a toughness that Cluaran had not seen before. He would do well enough.

Cluaran coaxed a spark from his fire-stone, lit a torch for himself and one for Ari, and led the way into the tunnel.

The dark closed in on him before he had gone five paces; too thick a blackness to be much disturbed by his little torch. He raised the stick higher and glanced over his shoulder. Edmund was just behind him, his face determined. The girl, Fritha, who came next, was almost lost in shadow, but Cluaran could see that she was walking quietly and did not seem about to panic. The other two could not be seen, but Ari's torch was a smoky flickering in the darkness behind. Cluaran thrust his own light ahead of him and pushed on. It did not illuminate much more than the next three steps, but he remembered the descent as almost straight, with no sudden drops – unless something had changed it. He had thought he knew what they would face down in the cave . . . but Eolande was there! He was well aware of her power. What might she use it for, if Loki had taken her? *And how was he able to take her?* a voice in his head asked; but he put that aside for now.

He set each foot down gently, keeping all his senses alert for traps. *Don't try to run!* he told himself. *Remember how long the way is – we have to be of some use when we get there.* But he could not stop his steps from speeding up. Behind him he heard Edmund and Fritha talking in low voices, and had a momentary urge to snap at them to be silent – but why? Loki would know they were coming. The chains might still be holding, down there in the fiery chamber, but he had long been able to send his mind out into the mountain, and far beyond it. Cluaran was only too well aware of that.

Edmund and Fritha fell silent after a while, as if the tunnel sucked away sound as well as light. The heat was beginning to creep over them. Cluaran's torch was smoking badly; he heard Edmund cough as a stream of smoke drifted sluggishly backwards. Next moment, the cloth he had wound about the stick came loose: an end trailed down, scattering sparks over his sleeve. Cluaran cursed, moving to beat them out – and the flame caught and ran along his arm; across his chest. In two heartbeats, his whole body was engulfed in fire.

He heard Edmund gasp; Fritha screamed, and he thought even Ari cried out. Ignoring the panicked beating of his heart, Cluaran closed his eyes. *No.* The heat he felt was no worse than before. But his mind was still howling at him that his body was burning . . .

'No!' he cried aloud, and opened his eyes. The hand that held the torch was lapped in flame; blistering, blackening; but he looked away from it, at the others. Their stricken faces were clearly visible in the red glare. All had leapt backwards, away from him; only Ari stood unmoving behind them.

'It's not fire!' Cluaran shouted. 'It's just seeming!' The raw horror on Edmund's and Fritha's faces had not changed. He looked down at his body. His chest was blazing as if his very heart were on fire. His hands were blackened claws. He turned his face away from them and walked briskly away down the tunnel. 'Come on!' he yelled, without turning his head. 'Would I be standing if this were real?'

There was still no move behind him. He darted a look backwards, and saw that the flames had spread with him. From the place where he had stood before, the tunnel was filled with fire. He took a deep breath and roared into it.

'*I'm not harmed!* Close your eyes, and come forward!'

They came to him through the fire. Edmund opened his eyes after the first step, looking about him in wonder as the unfelt flames licked at him. Fritha, her eyes screwed shut, held on to Edmund's cloak to follow him. It was Cathbar who seemed the most troubled: the captain marched forward, squinting through half-closed lids, but when he reached Cluaran his face was grey, the old burn-scars standing out lividly on his cheek and chin.

Ari came last, his torch held aloft, though its flame was lost in the fire all around him. And then the fire was gone like a candle snuffed out, and the blackness returned, so thick that it took long moments for the torch flames to be visible again. Cluaran glanced up at his own torch: the cloth was tightly secured around it, double-knotted with twine. The hand that held it was his own hand again, unmarked. The relief that washed over him took him by surprise. He waited for a moment, listening to Edmund's and Fritha's exclamations and nervous laughter and Cathbar's reassurances; then, when he was sure his voice would be steady, he called them to order.

'Loki plays tricks, remember? But he can't hurt us unless we let him, as you see. Now – we still have a long way to go.'

They set off again, and this time Cluaran did not try to pace them. They marched through the darkness until the nervous energy sparked by the fire began to wear off, their eyes slowly accustoming to the dim glow of the torches. When the others began to drop behind, taking off their cloaks in the growing heat, Cluaran slowed his pace a little, though he felt he could have gone on like this for longer.

They walked on unhindered until the red spark of the opening appeared in the distance. The torches were burning low by now, and Cluaran saw the faint red glow appearing on the walls with relief. Then, just as they were beginning to see the tunnel unaided, the ground dropped away a single step ahead of him.

'This is the cavern?' Fritha whispered.

The walls had given way too: they stood looking out on to a vast, empty chasm, lit by red fires a hundred feet below. There was nothing beyond; nothing but the dizzying drop.

'Not yet,' Cluaran said. 'Stay where you are.' His cloak was over his arm: he dropped it over the edge of the chasm and saw it fall, the fastening-pin flashing red, to vanish in the fires below. He knelt and stretched out a hand, closing his eyes tight. The stone floor was rough and warm beneath his hand, and there was the familiar material of the cloak, lying in a heap just beyond.

He stood, draping the cloak over his arm and extinguishing the torch; hearing the exclamations of alarm behind him.

'Edmund,' he called softly, 'take hold of my back, and have Fritha do the same to you. Form a chain, close your eyes again and walk when I do. Don't let go, and do not open your eyes, whatever happens. Is that clear?'

He took a moment to check that they had followed his instructions. Then, closing his own eyes and stretching out his hands to the walls on each side, he moved out over the abyss.

The stone walls were firm under his hands. The ground stayed beneath his feet, and Edmund shuffled behind him, one hand on each of Cluaran's sides. After a dozen paces Cluaran risked half-opening an eye. He was suspended in empty space; the walls abruptly vanished and for a hideous second his fingers could not feel the stone. Panic overtook him and he hurled himself sideways, clenching his eyes shut. His head collided painfully with the wall, and Edmund's hands were almost wrenched from his sides.

'Don't open your eyes!' he snapped, as if Edmund had disobeyed him. He moved on, clinging to the wall and feeling each step with agonising slowness, until his hands reached the opening, and his face felt the hot air that breathed through it. *You can stop your illusions now, monster!* he thought, savagely. *You have us before you.*

There were voices in his ears – real voices. He heard Elspeth, crying out in protest; and another voice, low, cool and painfully familiar.

Cluaran shook off Edmund's hands, and in two paces he

was in the cavern, its echoing spaces and red light calling back all the memories he had hoped so much to bury. He peered through the flames at the cavern's end: the prisoner was still in his shackles, shrunk to man-size. But there was someone with him. Across the river of fire, someone had charmed a frail bridge, almost eaten away already by the flames. Cluaran broke into a run, hardly hearing the cries of Edmund and the others behind him.

Elspeth stood as if turned to stone, gazing at the chained Loki. All the life in her body seemed to have gone into the sword, which twisted and writhed above her head like a living thing, blazing white. A cloud of after-images danced in the air around it. Eolande stood behind Elspeth, both her hands on the girl's sword arm, urging her towards the chained figure on the rock.

And as Cluaran rushed towards them, Loki turned his head to look him in the face, a figure of flame, yellow eyes flashing, his mouth stretching in a grin of ferocious joy.

Elspeth took a single step forward, and the woman guided her hand down – but not towards Loki's breast. The sword screamed as it sliced through the chains binding his feet – one, two! Cluaran was almost at the bridge as Eolande brought the blade up to free the prisoner's arms. Loki was on his feet, bound only by the one remaining chain at his neck. His smile broadened as he reached out towards Elspeth, and the flames around them roared upwards, hiding him from sight.

Howling wordlessly, Cluaran leapt into the trench, launching himself through the flames and feeling the last of the bridge crumbling beneath his feet. He threw himself on Elspeth and Eolande, hurling the girl to the ground and grasping the woman by both arms.

'Stop!' he gasped. 'Mother – what have you done?'

CHAPTER TWENTY-ONE

I have destroyed all I held dear.

My son burst in on us as Ioneth entered the sword. I had not known he was capable of such suffering. He will not speak to me again.

The sword is like no other. After it took Ioneth, it vanished, but I felt it in my hand, and feel it there still. Yesterday the Chained One called forth his rock dragon, and the sword sprang forth to meet it. Ioneth and I beat the dragon back; we saved many lives.

I am tired, and very old. But the battle is not over.

For a moment Elspeth lay where she was, her head spinning. Someone had burst through the flames shouting and stopped her from killing her father – no, from killing *Loki*. She opened her eyes and blinked in a glare of firelight. Flames danced near her face, scorching her. She pulled herself to her knees, gazing about her in confusion. Where was her father?

He had gone. A figure that was too tall to be her father stood before the rock, tethered to the stone by a single chain. He seemed to shift and flicker as she looked at him, almost as if he were burning. There was a voice in her head screaming at her, telling her she must do something, but she could not remember what it was, and could not make out the words.

In front of the chained figure, only a few paces away, Eolande stood like a stone, facing the man who had thrown Elspeth down. She saw, with a dull surprise, that it was Cluaran. What was he doing here? And had he just called Eolande 'mother'? He was holding the Fay woman by the shoulders, shaking her and shouting into her face.

'How could you do this?'

'But I have to free him.' Eolande's voice was bewildered. 'I have worked so long for this! Cluaran – do you not know your own father?'

NO! screamed the sword in Elspeth's head, and her gaze snapped to the chained figure at the rock. She could see his face clearly now: a handsome young man, his eyes slanted and flame-yellow. As she watched, his mouth turned up in a mocking smile.

Cluaran was staring at Eolande, still gripping her shoulders. 'Mother . . .' he said at last, his voice almost gentle, 'My father is dead. You know that.'

Eolande tried to pull away from him, shaking her head. Elspeth stared past them both, at the chained man. *My father is dead . . .*

Loki! The sword shrieked in her mind. *The deceiver! He must not trick you again. Kill him, now, while one chain remains!*

Elspeth found that she was on her feet. She took a step forward, then another, bringing her alongside Eolande. The Fay woman seemed not to notice her: she was talking, pleading with Cluaran, but Elspeth could no longer hear her.

Strike! the sword cried. *Close your eyes and strike!*

Over Eolande's shoulder, Cluaran threw Elspeth one glance of desperate appeal. *Please, kill him!*

The chained man at the rock smiled still wider. Elspeth looked full at the fiery, grinning face, no longer certain if the voice she heard was Ioneth's or her own. *He takes life, and gives back lies. KILL HIM!* And now she was darting forward, the sword blazing in her hand.

'Good. Good!'

Loki's voice rang out, rich and powerful as a bell, in the heartbeat before Elspeth reached him. It reverberated through the cavern, sounding in her very bones. (*No!* Ioneth screamed. *Don't listen!*)

Loki looked down at Elspeth, ignoring the sword, and reached out a hand to her. 'Come to me, child. I still have need of you.'

And he was her father again: on the day she first learnt to swim, his face blazing with love and pride as he held out his dripping arms to pull her up from the water.

Elspeth clenched her eyes shut. *Now!* Ioneth screamed, and

the sword surged in Elspeth hand as she leapt blindly forward to strike.

She felt the blade make contact, with a clash as if it struck sparks from stone. There was a cry of triumph filling her head, and all around her a howl, so shrill it could not be human.

Her enemy was standing before her, hands by his side, his candle-flame eyes wide with shock as he looked down at the long gash down his shoulder and chest.

Strike again! Ioneth's voice rang in her ears. *Strike now!* And Elspeth raised the blade and drove it straight at Loki's heart.

Loki was quicker. With the speed of a snake he darted aside and lunged at Elspeth, catching her sword hand and forcing the blade up between them. The smile had gone from his handsome face, and the yellow eyes blazed at her.

'Now,' he breathed, 'come to me.'

Ioneth's song of triumph had become a shriek of terror. A bolt of agony shot down Elspeth's arm, as if every nerve was being pulled from her.

Help me! Ioneth screamed through the roaring in her head. *Elspeth – hold on!* And she tried to pull back, to stand against the demon's force, though her arm was withering in the fire, and her eyes blinded by searing light.

There was a sound like a high, clear bell, or like a smith's hammer giving one final tap. The sword shuddered violently in her hands and shattered, fountaining into a million motes of light which winked around her before dissolving into the air. They faded, and faded, until there was nothing left but darkness.

Edmund had watched it all through the curtain of flame, standing with Cathbar and Fritha at the edge of the fiery river. He clenched both hands into fists as Elspeth ran forward, but did not dare to utter a sound. When his friend wounded Loki, then lunged at his heart, Edmund had wanted to shout in triumph – but the demon had caught Elspeth's hand, and a moment later the sword had burst into a glittering cloud, and vanished. It was not until he saw Elspeth fall to the ground that Edmund cried out. But there was nothing he could do.

Loki was glowing as if lapped in flames. His face convulsed in fury as he glared down at the motionless figure of Elspeth, his whole body seeming to swell with rage. The iron band around his neck, the only thing that still kept him tethered to the rock, swelled with him, and he raised his hands to tug at it.

'He's still bound!' Cathbar cried.

But Ari, beside him, groaned. 'No. That chain was fixed by a mortal man, Brokk. I saw him do it. The other chains were cast by gods, long before. That one alone was made anew during the last battle.' The pale man's voice was dull with despair. 'It will not hold!'

The wolfish grin was back on Loki's face as he turned to inspect the chain that linked the band to the rock.

Cluaran leapt to his feet, his dagger drawn in one last desperate attack, but Loki knocked him to the ground as casually as a man swatting a fly. The demon took up a double handful of the chain, strained for the space of a heartbeat, and broke the links. The clatter as the twisted metal fell on to the rock echoed around the cavern.

Loki stood for a moment more surveying them all: Elspeth and Cluaran on the ground; Eolande standing as if turned to stone, gazing at him; and the others, watching helplessly from beyond the burning river. He sighed, throwing his head back as if in ecstasy. A broad, delighted smile spread across his handsome face; spread until it was no longer handsome; the lips stretching too wide for a face to bear them; the teeth flashing sharp as a wolf's.

And then the whole face was growing. It filled Edmund's vision, eyes stretching like flames in a wind, the hair writhing and leaping like a bonfire. Edmund leapt back – the burning eyes seemed to be looking directly at him. Loki's body billowed upwards like smoke as he swept them an ironic bow. He turned and strode away down the river of fire, growing taller with each step, the rock on each side seeming to melt away before him.

Then there was only the red-lit stone, as solid as before, and an echo of mocking laughter.

So it's over, Edmund thought. *What will happen now?* Images flashed through his mind, of flame overwhelming the snow plains, of burning trees and houses. He forced the thoughts away. Elspeth was still lying on the rocky floor beyond the flames; a small, twisted figure, so still . . . *She can't be dead. She can't!*

Eolande had run to the edge of the burning river and was gazing down it, her face blank with disbelief. Cluaran was pulling himself to his feet, groaning. He looked at the empty chains dangling from the rock; he walked slowly to one of them and fingered the cut edge, as if to feel where the sword had sliced.

Behind him, Elspeth stirred, her empty right hand clutching the air. Edmund, watching, gave a cry of joy, and Cluaran turned to look at the girl. He bent over her hand, turning it in his own, and Edmund saw his face twist with grief. He lowered his head for a long moment. Then he lifted Elspeth in his arms and carried her to the wreck of the stone bridge.

'The girl needs aid,' he shouted. 'Ari, can you get us across?'

Edmund turned to Ari. 'What can I do?'

'Collect more stones,' Ari told him. 'Big ones – and hurry. We have to leave here.'

They used one loose rock to chip out another, passing them along to Fritha and Cathbar, who threw them into the fiery stream. It took longer without Eolande's charms; the Fay woman was wandering along the rock face, running her hands over the surface as if looking for an opening, oblivious to what the others were doing.

At length the flames were quelled enough to allow Cluaran across. He handed Elspeth to Cathbar, and looked back across the burning river. But Eolande seemed not to see or hear him, and after a moment's hesitation he turned back to the others.

Cathbar laid Elspeth gently on the rocky ground, rolling up his cloak for a pillow. Her hand was burned red, and her face was paler than Edmund had ever seen it. She hardly seemed to be breathing. He leant over her, searching for any stir of life.

'Don't die, Elspeth!' he whispered.

'She is strong, your friend.' Edmund looked up to see Cluaran's companion, Ari, beside him. The pale man bent over Elspeth, feeling for a pulse in her wrists. 'I have seen some among our people like this, when they escaped the hungry ghosts. Her spirit may yet return.'

Elspeth's chest was rising very slightly. As Edmund watched, her mouth opened and he heard a faint, rasping breath. 'You're safe now,' he told her, but there was no sign that she could hear him.

'So she'll recover,' Cluaran said to Ari. It was a statement, not a question, but the minstrel's face looked set and grim.

Ari hesitated before replying. 'I think so,' he said at last. 'But few who touch Loki come away unscathed.'

Cluaran nodded, his face unchanging. 'And the sword is lost,' he said.

'I'm sorry, Cluaran.'

For a moment Edmund saw pity on Ari's face – pity and grief. *Why grieve for a sword?* he wondered. *When Elspeth could still be in danger?*

Cluaran was gazing bleakly back at the rock where Loki had been chained. Edmund, following his gaze, saw that Eolande was still standing at the rock, muttering to herself and weeping softly. Cluaran made no move towards her.

'Cluaran,' Edmund said hesitantly, 'is Eolande really your mother?'

The minstrel nodded. 'Yes. My mother . . . and Loki's slave.' His voice was very soft, and he did not turn to look at Edmund. 'He tricked her: it was my father she saw in those chains. He must have told her he was Brokk, and that she could free him with the enchanted sword.' He ran a hand over his face. 'And so she sent Torment to wreck Elspeth's father's ship, and then to carry the two of you here from Venta Bulgarum. She even sent books to Orgrim, that would help him serve Loki's dark purpose. She did all this for the sake of a man who has been dead one hundred years.'

For the first time he turned to show his face, and Edmund flinched at the raw sorrow in his eyes and the line of his mouth. 'Try not to hate her too much. You can see he has driven her mad.' He went back to staring at Eolande as she felt her way along the rock. 'All those years,' he muttered. 'All that time she stayed here alone with him.'

Cathbar's voice behind them made Edmund jump. 'Should we not be leaving here? The fire is growing.'

He was right, Edmund realised. The air in the cavern was heavy with the smell of burning, and the ground beneath him was hot through the soles of his boots. The black walls seemed to smoke as if the rock was scorched. And all around them, under the ground and behind the walls, was a low rumbling, growing louder and deeper.

'Loki is waking the volcano,' said Ari.

The fiery river that separated them from the rock was over-flowing its bounds; as Edmund stared in alarm, a trickle of molten stone spilled out along one wall, and the flames rising from the surface rose higher, beginning to overwhelm the rickety bridge. Cluaran leapt up and was across the stones in two strides. Eolande had stopped inspecting the rock surface and was staring down the river of flames to where Loki had vanished.

'Brokk, where have you gone?' she sobbed. 'Why have you left me again?' She did not turn when her son reached her.

'No ... no ...' she mumbled, as Cluaran dragged her towards the bridge. 'I must wait for Brokk. He will come back to me. Leave me!'

Cluaran hauled his mother over the shifting stones and flung her into Cathbar's arms, ignoring her cries. The flames closed in on the minstrel as he threw himself after her, catching and spreading up one of his sleeves; then the other. Not an illusion this time, but real, burning. Edmund and Fritha rushed to help him beat out the flames, while Ari lifted Elspeth. She moaned faintly, and hung limp in his arms.

'I'll lead,' the pale man said. 'Edmund, Fritha, light the torches and follow.'

As Edmund gingerly held his torch to the leaping flames at

the edge of the river, he saw a hair-thin line of red at the base of the rock beyond it. He did not stop to see if the crack was growing: he knew it meant that the mountain was about to burst open in a tide of burning liquid rock.

Ari had already entered the tunnel with Fritha close behind him; the smoky glow of her torch was diminishing into the darkness ahead. Edmund cast one more look around the cavern before following them. The flames leaping from the fiery river were a solid wall now, taller than a man, and the heat from them hit him in the face like a slap. Cluaran and Cathbar were half-dragging, half-carrying Eolande away from the flames, while she struggled and held out her arms to the now obscured rock. Glowing tendrils snaked across the ground as if pursuing them.

Edmund turned and plunged into the tunnel. Eolande's cries echoed in the close space as she was dragged after him. And then the rumbling behind them became a roaring, and the ground shook under their feet as they ran.

CHAPTER TWENTY-TWO

Loki will break his chains again, as the Fay foretold. Even now his power shows itself: the mountain glows; the dragons will fly again. But the sword that can kill him is forged.

Old as I am, it is my task to kill him. I will go alone. If I cannot pierce his flesh, I can bring his accursed mountain down around his ears. The sword will cut through stone, at least.

To Eolande, whom I abandoned; to Cluaran, my Starling; whom I betrayed: my love and sorrow. May you live long and safe, and may you come one day to forgive me.

Elspeth stirred. There was a dull, regular pounding in her ears; she floated in the midst of it, bodiless. Walls of grey ice rose all around her, but it was hot; a stream of fire flowed through the cave's centre, its flickering red light dancing over the ice walls and rock floor.

But where was the great rock beyond the fire – the rock

where Loki was chained? She had been fighting Loki, Elspeth remembered: she had wounded him; and then . . .

Where was she? This place was smaller than the cavern beneath *Eigg Loki*, and it was full of metallic din. But she knew she had been here before. And then she saw the forge set up over the fiery stream, and she remembered.

The old smith, Brokk, was shaping the sword. He worked as if there were nothing in the world but the hammer and the glowing strip beneath it, his gaze fixed on the white-hot metal. The clangs from his hammer were as regular as heart-beats. And she could feel her heart beating now . . . not her heart, but that of the woman, watching . . .

She stood pressed against the ice wall: her back chilled; the heat of the fire in front eating into her skin through the thin shift. She would have to go closer to it in a few moments; the stone and metal would become part of her, and the fire too.

The demon murdered my brothers and my father, she reminded herself. *He killed my whole race. And I can stop him for ever . . .*

When Brokk called to her, she stepped forward without hesitation. The pain as she caught hold of the blade was beyond imagining: she felt her skin melting; the heat scorching through her veins; burning her very heart . . . And then she was ice again, whirling motes in the air, and the pain was far away. Nothing was solid: nothing but the blade, which glowed like living crystal; her only centre; pulling her in.

Suddenly something was calling her back. With an effort,

she opened the eyes that had been hers, and looked at the young man shouting outside the circle of light.

It was Cluaran, her beloved, his face riven with sorrow.

She had never lied to him, but she had not told him why she was coming here. He would have done everything in his power to stop her

'Take me instead!' he was sobbing. She felt a rush of tenderness for him. If she could only have made him understand how important this was; the countless people their sacrifice would save. But she only had the strength to murmur a few words of love and farewell.

Her body faded behind her as the sword received her. She was a weapon from this moment; her whole being bent on a single purpose: to destroy, and to save what was left of her people. But his last words stayed with her, filling her with a pain she had thought she would never feel again: sorrow, and loss.

Ioneth! Don't leave me . . .

Elspeth opened her eyes with a start. She was bent double over something warm and animal-smelling and being carried, fast and jerkily. She was draped over a horse's back, and the whiteness jolting past beneath her was snow. She tilted her head to see the horse's brown neck and head, and the figure of Cluaran, leading it on a short rein over the snow fields. A wave of remembered sorrow overtook her as she looked at his bent head. She had left him . . . *no*, Ioneth had left him. He

had watched as she gave herself to the sword, and he was pow-
erless to stop her. *Is he still grieving?* she wondered. Her hand
hurt, and another question came to her: what had happened
to the sword? She could not remember clearly what had happened in the cave under the mountain: she had struck at her
enemy; she had wounded him, surely . . . but after that came
a blank. Had Ioneth fulfilled her purpose?

Did I kill Loki?

Someone squeezed her hand. Out of the corner of her eye
she saw that it was Edmund, his face grimy and his fair hair
matted with soot and ash.

'Edmund,' she tried to say. 'What happened in the cave?'
The words would not come out clearly, and she could not be
sure he had understood. He seemed about to speak, but then
just gave her a lopsided smile and pressed her hand again.

Somehow, his presence reassured her. The world was not at
an end yet. She tried to smile back at him, found even that
too much effort, and fell asleep again.

When she awoke, the motion had stopped. She was lying
on the ground beneath a tree, swaddled in furs, with other
trees around her. Snow lay on the ground in the gaps between
overhanging branches, and she shivered in spite of her fur
wraps. Through the tall trunks came slanted red rays of sunlight: whether early or late in the day, she could not say.
Edmund leant beside her, grey with exhaustion. Cluaran
was sitting against the tree next to hers, talking quietly to
Ari, who knelt near him. To the other side of her, Fritha and

Cathbar lay stretched on their cloaks, sleeping deeply. And further away, crouching among the trees like a hunted animal, was Eolande. Elspeth hardly recognised the Fay woman at first: she seemed to have shrunk. Her glossy hair fell in matted straggles about a face which seemed sunken in on itself; her eyes were haunted and she stared straight ahead of her, ignoring the others.

Elspeth wondered what ailed her . . . and what other thing was wrong. Her friends were all here, and apart from Eolande, they seemed to be unharmed. So why did she feel that someone was missing? Why this terrible sense of loss?

And then she felt the emptiness in her right hand.

Ioneth!

She must have cried out, for suddenly Edmund was leaning over her, his hand on her arm. 'It's all right,' he said. 'You're safe, Elspeth – we all are.' But the tension in his face belied his words.

'No!' she said urgently. 'It's not all right. Edmund – what happened? What happened to Loki? And the sword?'

He only shook his head, not meeting her gaze. Elspeth tried to pull herself up against the tree trunk and found she could manage it without too much dizziness. 'Tell me!' she insisted. Terror made her voice hoarse. '*Please*, Edmund!'

'Loki is free,' Edmund said softly. 'You . . . the sword . . . Eolande made you cut his chains. The sword has gone. You wounded him with it, and it seemed to . . . burst.' His eyes were full of misery. 'I'm so sorry, Elspeth.'

The memory came flooding back. Her father's face, his voice . . . Eolande's cold hands on hers . . . and the demon's laughter as he took the life of the sword. She wanted to raise her head and howl, but no sound would come.

Cluaran had risen and come over to her. His face looked pinched, and he huddled in his cloak as if cold to his bones. 'How much do you remember?' he asked quietly.

Elspeth must have revealed her horror and guilt in her face because he knelt and took her by the shoulders with a gentleness she had not seen in him before. 'It was not your fault, Elspeth. Eolande, my mother, betrayed you; betrayed us all. She tricked you into cutting his chains; all but the last, and that he broke himself.'

'I thought he was my father,' Elspeth said.

Cluaran nodded, his face drawn with grief. 'He has always been the trickster. He deceived Eolande as well. And the one he could not deceive, the sword . . . he has taken her life to feed his power. He will be as strong as he ever was.'

'We've been running from the mountain all day,' Edmund added. 'It's been spitting out fire. Cluaran says it will soon be molten rock – it could cover the whole of the snow fields. But we should be far enough away to be safe now. Safe from the mountain, at least . . .' His voice tailed off unhappily.

'Brokk . . .' Eolande's voice came to them from where she was slumped. She spoke dreamily, almost in a singsong, without looking at them. Cluaran whirled to face her.

'My father is *dead* – don't you understand? How could you

let Loki trick you? You had such wisdom, such knowledge of truth and lies. How could you do this?

'He did *not* die!' Eolande's eyes came back into focus, for a moment there was a flash of the proud woman she might have been once. 'No one saw him die! I waited for him long after you and all the rest had abandoned him in the mountain. And at last I found him, chained. And I worked to free him – how could I do less?'

'It was a hundred years ago!' said Cluaran, his voice strained and desperate. 'He was already an old man when he went into the mountain. How could you think he would still be alive?'

'It was an enchantment.' Eolande's voice had softened. 'I despaired for a long time. But then I heard Brokk's voice, and saw him, and spoke to him. He was young and beautiful as when I first knew him. But he suffered and wasted in the chains! And then he told me I could free him, if I really wanted.'

'And you did all he asked!' Cluaran said hotly. 'You sowed treachery and murder; you sent the dragon to wreck ships and kidnap children. Do you think my father would have asked that of you? He gave his life to defeat Loki!' His voice broke. 'And so did Ioneth. Now all their sacrifice has been for nothing.'

'*Ioneth.*' Eolande's voice was bitter as poison. 'It was she who drove you both away from me. From the time you met her you would look at no one else. And later, when the sword

225

was found, and Brokk was not, you chose to go away, to follow the sword. You would not stay for your father . . . or your mother.'

'I should have come back for you,' Cluaran said, very softly. 'But you should have known that there was nothing left for you here!'

'Brokk was here,' Eolande insisted. 'And now I have freed him, he will come back to me.'

'No,' said Cluaran, and the way he spoke told of a hundred years of grieving. 'Brokk is dead. You freed Loki.'

There was a silence. Eolande's eyes were dark as she stared back at him.

'If that is so,' she said, 'if Brokk is truly gone, then let the world turn to dust. What do I care?' She stared ahead of her, dead-eyed, and said no more.

Elspeth had listened with pity at first, but then with growing anger. All their loss, all the long journeying – the loss of the sword – were all the fault of this woman! And now, to dismiss the fate of the whole world! But she saw Cluaran's face, and kept silent.

'She does not know what she's saying,' Ari said quietly to Cluaran. 'Blame Loki for this, Cluaran, not your mother.'

'You are right,' Cluaran said heavily. 'How long will it be, do you think, Ari, before he regains his full power? Until he can burn the world with a thought?'

Ari did not answer at once. 'He drew power from the sword's death,' he said at last. 'But he could not take the sword for his own use, nor take Elspeth's spirit. And that band your father closed round his neck – that was still there when he left us. There is poison to him in the iron: it will prevent him from doing all that he wishes. If I were to guess, I'd say we have until he looses the final band.'

So there may still be hope? Elspeth thought. *Or would be, if the sword had not shattered.* She looked down at her burned hand. A dark-red band ran across the palm, and it throbbed with pain as it had when the sword first came to her.

Her arm was throbbing, too. She had felt nothing there a moment ago.

Think, Elspeth – what happened when the sword broke? Loki had tried to take it from her. Her arm had burned as he wrenched out each nerve that clung to it. And Ioneth had been pulled with it. She could still hear the terrified voice: *Help me! Hold on!*

And she *had* held on. Loki had not taken the sword from her; it had shattered. So where was Ioneth?

Elspeth looked down at her right hand. If she concentrated, could she still feel the hilt there? Maybe . . . maybe there was something.

Ioneth! she called inside her head. *Ioneth – can you answer me?*

And there was the voice, hovering on the very edge of thought, so faint she could hardly hear it, but as familiar to her as her own heartbeat.

Elspeth . . .

Elspeth leapt to her feet, ignoring Edmund's startled cry. 'She's still here!' she gasped.

'Who is?' Edmund said – and stopped as a livid yellow light flashed beyond the trees, and the ground shook beneath them.

Fritha burst through the trees, a bundle of sticks under her arm. 'You must come!' she said breathlessly. 'The mountain burns . . .'

They followed her to the edge of the trees. The sun was setting between the mountains – but a brighter glow had burst from the top of *Eigg Loki*. Fire was pouring down the mountain's side, driving the snow before it in clouds of vapour. Even so far away, Elspeth thought she could hear the ice of the lake cracking, and see the spirits writhing in the black water as it hissed up into steam. There were few remaining lights from fishermen's fires – some went out abruptly as tiny black figures were pitched into the lake or scuttled away across the snow.

Edmund was gazing away from the lava stream, towards the foot of the mountain a little to the left. No, not gazing: his eyes were closed, and his lips moved urgently. There was a sudden disturbance at the mountain's foot. What had looked like a low snowbound hill slowly heaved itself up and stretched to reveal a long neck and head – then wings, surely bigger than were possible on a living creature. A white dragon!

'How . . . ?' Elspeth gasped. The creature must be bigger than Torment – half the size of the mountain!

The dragon lumbered away from the fire, flapping ponderously until it gained the air. For an instant, its scales were lit by the brilliant glares of sunset and flames, and a glittering stream of water flowed from its tail as it swooped over the volcano. Then the creature wheeled slowly in the sky, becoming black against the fire's glow, and soared away to the west, losing itself in the setting sun.

Edmund let out a sigh of relief, and Elspeth saw to her astonishment that he was smiling. 'I'll tell you about her when there's more time,' he said. The others had already vanished back into the trees, and they ran to join them.

Cathbar was on his feet and ready to go. 'If you'll take us to the nearest village,' he said to Cluaran, 'I'll see to it that young Elspeth and Edmund get home. They've done more than enough.'

Cluaran was already nodding when Elspeth spoke.

'No. It's not over yet.'

They all turned to look at her as she rushed on, her words falling over each other. 'Edmund – Cluaran – she's not dead. Ioneth's not dead! I can still feel her, inside my head. She's *here*, Cluaran!'

The minstrel flinched as if she had hit him – but his look was one of dismay, his gaze involuntarily flicking sideways to where Eolande stood, passive and blank-faced.

'It's *not* one of Loki's tricks!' Elspeth insisted impatiently. 'He plays with your eyes – but I can't see her. I just know her voice. And I can *feel* her.' She went to him, taking his hand and willing him to trust her.

Edmund believed her, she could see that at once. Cathbar looked troubled. But Cluaran stared at her speechlessly, his face torn between hope and despair. The voice was in her head again, fainter than a whisper: *Yes. Tell Cluaran he must remember . . . I never died.*

'She tells Cluaran to remember that she never died,' Elspeth repeated, and watched as the spark of hope on the minstrel's face became a blaze. She could see the belief in Ari's expression too – but the pale man shook his head slowly.

'There's little hope, even so,' he said. 'Loki is no longer bound, and even if he lacks part of his strength, he can still destroy – and he will, I fear.' He gestured to the red light growing behind them, clearly visible through the trees. 'And we no longer have the sword.'

'We'll find it again.' Elspeth was surprised by the confidence in her own voice. 'I was the one who freed Loki. It's for me to capture him again.' She felt once more the faint presence in her head, giving her strength and courage. 'And this time, I will kill him.'

EPILOGUE

The King's Rede at Winchester was in full session for the first time in four years: its last members had all returned from exile, Aagard among them. His beard was whiter than when the Rede had seen him last, and his scarlet robes more ragged, but every man there, from the king down, heaved a sigh of relief to see him restored to his rightful place.

Ill-founded relief, Aagard thought as he looked at the expectant faces before him. For an unworthy instant he wished that Godric had not given him the spell books, and that he had never used the divination charm he had found there: it was hard to return in triumph, only to bring the worst of news. But the kingdoms would have to work together now as never before: it was no time to despair. Not yet.

'Masters,' he announced, 'I am glad and honoured to be here again. But I wish I could mark my return with happier tidings.'

Ah – the hall erupted into whispers. This was not wholly

unexpected, then, and Aagard was glad to see that some among the Rede had been prepared. Even so, his next words brought stunned silence.

'I have learned that the Chained One is chained no longer. He has escaped from the mountain where he was imprisoned. We must prepare for battle.'

Through the cries of horror and alarm, Godric's thin old voice asked, 'And the children?'

'The minstrel Cluaran saved them,' Aagard told him. It was the one ray of hope he possessed. And even here, there was something ominous to add. 'They remain our best hope of destroying the monster. But . . .' he heard murmurs of alarm building as he spoke, '. . . it seems the girl, Elspeth, tried to kill him and failed. She escaped, but the sword was lost.'

The groans rose all about him now, and he saw stark despair on many faces. 'There is still hope!' he insisted. 'Our fathers defeated Loki, and we can defeat him again. We must prepare ourselves, and we must stand together!'

He managed to rally them. Those who were wealthy promised horses and armour, and hurried to prepare them. Others, with friendly links to the neighbouring kingdoms, would leave that night with gifts and messages of goodwill. Every man went home to find his sword or his bow, and by evening the town was full of planning and activity.

Aagard stood behind the great hall, watching nervous townsmen queuing to practise swordsmanship with the king's soldiers. *Should I have kept the children here?* he wondered for the hundredth time, as he watched the inexpert men hacking at straw targets. *If I had done things differently, Loki might still be chained.*

But for how long? Sooner or later he would have escaped, and it would have come to this. Either Elspeth and her friends will find a way to destroy him, or he will destroy us. All the mortal world.

He looked towards the north, seeing in his mind's eye a red glow on the horizon – a great wave of fire, waiting to engulf the world.

'Let them find a way,' he whispered.

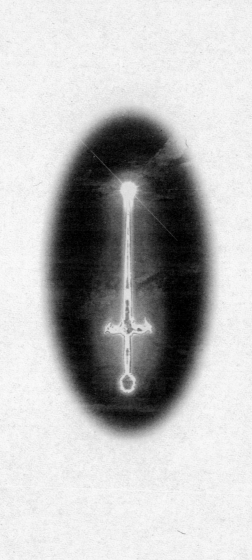